# BLOOD MEDICINE

## THOMAS TIMMINS

*Disclaimer*

*The author admits to taking a decade-long trip through the humid world of tofu making and marketing. He met countless inspired, industrious, good and eccentric people as he and his cohorts transformed soybeans into food for human beings. While some may wish to attribute familiar identities to some of the characters, living or dead, this is not a memoir. It is a work of fiction, arising from the author's imagination. Like all tall tales, it has at best a metaphoric relationship with what we perceive as the everyday world. If you find truth and pleasure in this book, they are yours to enjoy. That would make the author happy as the tofu master who, after stirring endless circles in a cauldron of hot soymilk, whips up a tasty batch of tofu he can serve to the world.*

*ACKNOWLEDGEMENTS:*

Joe Timmins, David Grant, Angela Borda, Nancy Shobe, Barbara Sachs, Judith Rubenstein, Amy Swisher, Thomas Dudley all had sensitive and caring hands in the making of this book. Without Judith Roberts, Richard and Kathy Leviton, Madeleine Fox, Jon Lee, Vinny Natale, Maggie Stebbins, Cory Greenberg, Donnie Nelson, Mary Houghton and hundreds of crew members and thousands of imaginative and intrepid tofu aficionados, the author could never have made the astonishing journey from soybean slinger to tofu tale teller. I thank each one of you.

# Contents

# Prologue

### Promotional Brochure
### from the American Tofu Company

# The Year of the Monkey

This is the year to say "Yes!" and expect miracles. Mimic the agile Monkey who won't stop till he swings from every branch and tests every angle. You'll land on your feet with a happy surprise in your hands and a smile on your face.

Enjoy this year as one big poker game. The one who gets the best deal will be the one who outsmarts the other. If you lose a hand, laugh. Monkeys shrug off their mistakes and find amusement everywhere.

Don't even try to keep track of who's ahead: the Monkey's left hand rarely knows what the right hand is up to. Not to worry—it's a year of huge rewards.

Help comes from the oddest places. Astonishing gifts arrive by coincidence, even from your enemies. Go ahead, say "Yes, Yes, Yes!" Be unpredictable, stretch and swing far. Have fun and you can leave the low-hanging fruit for the groundlings. Seriously, it's playtime.

*From The Year of the Monkey*
*Chinese New Year Promotional Brochure*
*American Tofu, Inc., Clement, New York*
*www.AmericanTofu.com*

# Chapter One

## *Becky MacDaniel*

# MY "BIG 3–0"

I jumped into his car as excited and happy as I'd ever been. He kissed me quick and bit my lip. He smelled like he'd put away as many Margaritas as I had.

It's sad or crazy or love, but every time I see him, I can't resist touching him. I shouldn't, but ... Like I can't control myself. He's not good for me, I know. But what else can I do?

We drove out of town, down a gravel road that followed the river, bumping along under a forest canopy drizzling with moonlight, my fingers caressing his bare hairy arm. Warm breeze from the river seeped into the car as we crept lights out toward wherever we were going.

What a birthday today. First, a surprise breakfast made with all the love my kids could give their mom. Lumpy pancakes and soggy bacon all drowned in maple syrup, just the way I like it. And perfect coffee—half milk, half sugar.

Then, tonight, thirty rowdy friends at my house ringing in my big 3-0. Nobody will ever forget that party, even if I did send everybody home early. They all believed my excuse that I had to be at work by four.

Now, celebrating in the full moon night with him. We might stay up all night. Before we climbed out of the truck, I touched his cheek and asked, "Don't you feel like a fish tonight?"

Wrinkling his nose, he said, "Not really." He raised his thick eyebrows and poked his fingers at my ribs. "More like a stallion."

I caught his fingers in my fists and held them in mid-air. "No, seriously. See those shadows? How they wiggle between the moon-beams? Like we're sitting in a three-dimensional fish net made of light and dark."

He grunted, "Yeah," and that's all, like he had something else on his mind. I knew what that was.

I uncapped my thermos of frozen margaritas and we sat drinking and toasting each other. Before long, we started laugh-ing and shrieking like idiots. We'd both had plenty to drink before we came out to the river.

We hopped down the root-stairs on the riverbank and stood in the pale shade of an enormous oak.

"Let's cross the river," he said. "I want to give you a present in style."

"I have a present for you, too," I whispered, kissing his ear.

He ogled my breasts like he always did and said, "I bet you do." I slapped his cheek, maybe a little too hard. He smiled. "Not that, " I said.

A jumble of rocks and boulders lay exposed above the shal-low August stream. "It looks slippery," I said.

"That's shadows, not water. I can cross with my eyes closed."

My feet stayed planted so he pointed across the water. "See that patch of moonlight? I want to see my princess dressed in just her new present."

He dug into his pants pocket and brought out a velvety little box. Flipping the lid back, he showed me two tiny green jewels glowing like stars in his moonlit hand. I reached for them, but he shut the lid and stuffed the box back into his pocket.

"That's all you want me to wear?" I couldn't believe he'd buy me something so expensive.

"You don't need anything else." He held out his arms. "Jump on. I'll carry you over."

"Like a groom?"

"Like a stallion."

We laughed until we bent over, bouncing off each other. I leapt up and swung my legs around his waist. Embracing his neck with both arms, I threw my head back and howled.

"Mmmm. You're heavy," he said, adjusting his grip. "Too much cake?"

"You're weak." I teased him back. I love those extra-strong stringy muscles in his arms and back.

He threw me up into a moonbeam slanting through the trees and flipped me around and settled me across his arms where I lay like a bride.

"Nobody ever called me weak before." Laughing, he tossed me up and down as he stretched his leg across the gap between the shore and a flat boulder in the river. Stopping on a flat boulder near the middle of the river, he slipped a little and hugged me tight to his chest while he stopped, regaining his balance.

I kissed him on the nose. "These rocks. Watch out. They're slippery." He didn't move for a moment. "Are you awake?" I said.

In answer, he nibbled my neck and mumbled, "Gotta be careful of moss. It bites."

Placid water trickled around luminous round rocks that lay scattered randomly between the banks the way my daughter drops biscuits onto a baking sheet. Below the surface, sharp rocks and pebbles fluttered like leaves in a breeze.

"Let me down. I can walk." I arched my back, trying to twist out of his arms.

"Hey, stop that. I got you."

"I want down."

"Quit wiggling like that, I might drop you."

I straightened my legs and pushed against his chest with the heels of my palms.

"Take it easy," he said, swaying back and forth. "please."

"Let go. You're too soused to carry me."

He took another step. As his foot touched down, he wobbled, stretched between two rocks.

"You want down? Be careful." My toes touched the boulder while he held onto my shoulders. He lost his balance and his leg skidded out and shot across the rock. His hands flew apart, flailing, he tipped backwards, my body slid away.

He shouted, "Becky! No! Becky!"

He tried to catch me, but when his fingers clutched at my back, I fell, face-first, through a moonbeam, into dark ... the rock ... oh ...

# Chapter Two

## *Charlie Greer*

# DEATH SPEAKS ALL LANGUAGES

*midnight phone ringing*
*who else but Benko?*
*the call that shattered my dream*

I was sailing in the Caribbean. Warm silky water flowed between my toes as I lay dangling my feet in a turquoise sea. Playful steel drum melodies drifted across the yacht from the Jamaican group playing on the stern, lolling me into euphoria.

Without warning, the wind shifted. The boat shuddered and the sail whipped, cracking the air inches from my head. The drums clanged, showering sharp, cold notes into my naked ears.

The phone rang four times before Nora got it.

"Charlie, wake up. It's Benko."

"What time is it?"

"Three fifty two."

She poked me in the shoulder with the phone.

"OK. OK."

I took the phone. Nora usually slept through middle-of-thenight calls from my tofu factory, but she woke up for this one. Her intuition must have told her that this was that dreaded call everybody gets sometime.

Benko wouldn't call if it was just a brown-out or production error. He was the best production manager I'd ever had and I totally trusted his judgment. I figured it wasn't a tragedy, because the police come to your door to tell you about that.

"Charlie," Benko growled in his heavy Russian accent, "Trouble, we got. Big."

"What's up, Benko? It's four in the morning." Half-asleep, I felt more annoyed than worried.

"Better get over here. Little problem it's not. Too much for me. I don't know what to do."

"Slow down. I can't understand you."

"Sorry. Cops. Cops I called." His normally confident voice trembled, frightening me. Sometimes I'm just paranoid, always worried about someone behind my back, but this time my radar was right.

"Somebody died."

"My God. Who?"

"Good-looking redhead? Becky. Cook, you know."

I jumped up out of bed. "What? What? Shit? Damn! How? God!"

Her eyes wide, Nora asked, "What?"

"Something bad happened at the factory."

I spoke into the phone.

"Benko, where is she?"

"Right here. I'm looking at body. Laying on floor by big tank."

"I'm out the door. Leave everything alone."

"Don't worry, Charlie. I got all covered."

Flashing blue and red lights, a patrol car and an ambulance idled in front of the American Tofu Company. The colors of blood pulsed in and out of the low office building's windows. The three-story factory loomed overhead, pale and gleaming in the security lights.

I approached the cop at the front door. "I'm the owner. Let me in." He started to ask me something but I rushed past him.

I ran through the dim offices lit only by streetlights shining in the windows and opened the swinging doors to the plant and smelled the musty odor of soybeans cooking. The scent distracted me for a second with a sense of comforting normalcy—the tofu factory chugging along.

On the far side of the fluorescence-bleached production room, another cop, some EMTs, my production manager Benko, and the half-dozen or so morning production workers dressed in white uniforms and caps stood in a circle staring at a body on the green floor. No one spoke. Steam billowed against the slick walls of the processing room where rows of tall, stainless steel caldrons and pipes glistened. Every few seconds, the tofu machinery pumped out loud booms followed by rhythmic hisses in the otherwise silent factory

The dead woman sprawled on the tile. It was Becky Mac-Daniel, a woman too familiar, intimately familiar, but nobody else was aware of that, I hoped. Seeing her there lying dead on the floor weakened my knees.

Water from the processing area flowed constantly across the green production room tiles. It pooled against one side of the body . I stared at her hand as the fingers bobbed up and down. Chilly water soaked my pants from my knees down to my socks.

*Tough luck, Greer. You should have known better than to fish off the company pier .*

I know. I know. My personal Jiminy Cricket never lets me off the hook. I can't shut him up, even if I try.

"Becky," Benko said in his gravely tones. "Morning shift bean cook." He put his arm around my shoulder.

"I see that." My neck relaxing against the grip of his muscular fingers. "Jesus, Benko. Your goddam accent on the phone confused me. I thought you said our chef—Gen, Genevieve."

"Shit, Charlie. Becky I said. Becky."

I shrugged off his arm and shouted. "Christ, Benko. You almost gave me a heart attack. I thought it was Genevieve." Genevieve O'Connor—we all depended on her to make the sales that paid the bills. Everyone knew how devoted I was to her.

One of the EMT's or cops mumbled, "He thought it was somebody else."

Good, they see it as a simple accident. That we can handle. I knelt down on the wet floor next to the body, my staged relief that it wasn't Genevieve fading in the harsh light of the dead Becky laid out on the floor

I wanted to pick Becky up and carry her out into the night and send everybody home and start the night over. Go back to the time before the company party months ago when I drove her home when she was drunk and I stayed too long.

She was the prettiest tofu worker in the company, but lying dead, she had the swollen face of a teenager who spent too much time in front of the TV set nibblng chips and chocolate.

*Greer, you've got ice in your veins. You'll need it now. You're in for nothing but pain.*

Sometimes you have to be cold. Don't need to get distracted by the pain, mine or anybody's. Benko squatted down beside me.

"Checking beans in tank, she slipped on platform." Keeping his voice low. "Knocked her head on the edge of tank. She had big birthday party last night. Could be she's still drunk this morning? Everything else in the factory ship-shop-shape. Right?"

"Thanks, Benko. You're probably right. All the cleanup records straight?" I stared at him hard. He had to make sure our records were in order. A blizzard of investigations would come our way police, state worker health and safety board, state food manufacturing inspectors, insurance companies.

Benko nodded at me. "Records in good shape. I make sure."

I nodded and exhaled for the first time since his call. He'd handle it.

The young policeman squatted beside me. He held his hat in his hand. "You the boss?"

"Yeah."

"Chief Buhrman's on his way. We gotta investigate."

"Sure. We don't have many accidents. My God, we have safety training. This is awful." Tears began to leak down my cheeks, surprising me with their volume and warmth. With the cop beside me, I said to Benko, "I thought she worked on the loading dock?"

"First week on new job. She wanted out of warehouse. So try cooking I told her. Chen found her upside down in tank. Called me." He nodded toward Chen, the tofu maker we'd hired from our New York City network of Chinese migrant workers. "Pump wouldn't draw beans so he checked tank. There she was. Head stuck in drain. He dragged her out. Called me. Like crazy man I ran here."

Empty-headed, I stared at the body. The shadow of black bra and panties on pink skin showed through her soaked uniform. A wave of dizziness rolled through me. After less than an hour of sleep, I'd raced here, my adrenaline pumping and blood sugar going nuts.

"Cops I call from home," Benko added. "I run here hoping she's knocked out maybe. Right away I see she's dead so I call you."

Benko had followed proper protocol. Thank God for him. His cool head hadn't failed me yet. He handled problems easily, fixed any machine, got production done on schedule and within budget. A good-looking guy, he smiled a lot, charmed me when he first stepped into my office, grinning like a kid. He reminded me of me if I were a mechanic. He could handle seventy production workers like they were his little kids. Especially the women, most of our crew.

I glanced up at Chen, the somber Chinese worker, for confirmation of Benko's story. His English almost non-existent, he shrugged. His whites were pressed and clean, except for a tan smudge across his chest. He must have crushed beans against himself when he dragged Becky out of the tank.

The other Chinese and the Latino production workers avoided my eyes, not wanting to volunteer any information, in English, Chinese, or Spanish.

But death speaks all languages. At that minute, everybody in the room was reading everybody else's mind. I emptied my mind of any thoughts about Becky, except the fact that she was dead and I was the boss and I had to keep myself and everybody else under control.

# Chapter Three

## *Charlie*

# DOUBLE MURDER?

*buried in soaking beans,*
*she forgot to wash her hands—*
*bloody fingernails*

The afternoon after Becky died, Police Chief Aaron Buhrman asked to see me in my office at the factory. "Got some pretty serious questions for you. Can't do it on the phone. You available now?"

My heart nearly stopped. Did he find something? I distracted myself with making phone calls to assure some of our vendors that all was all right with American Tofu, sad, but we'd bumble through, doing our best for the family and our employees.

By nine this morning, the street in front of the factory was jammed with vans, cars, pickups, and journalists insisting on talking with me. Channel 13 and Channel 10 and three other channels, reporters from five radio stations—even the university station every newspaper from Syracuse to Buffalo including *The Shoppers* clamored to get me to say something I'd regret.

I'll never know how, but that day's *New York Daily News* online led with a sickening headline "Suspicious Death in Upstate Tofu Factory." Rumors flew among our customers and competitors. Several of my friendliest competitors had called me to "express concern" about what this scandal-mongering would do to our sales. I even got a call from Xanadu Tofu in the Bay Area. Messages swamped the company's Facebook page. I considered taking it down.

I hoped the story would become a simple industrial accident before the *Enquirer* published something humiliating and sensational about us. I prayed that in a day or two, TV news would squeeze all the family tragedy they could out of the death and give up its coverage of American Tofu.

Despite the storm of bad publicity, my business mind wondered if, after the media calmed down, the constant repetition of American Tofu in the news would have a positive effect on sales. The old saying, any publicity is good publicity. I hoped so.

Genevieve O'Connor, my faithful and brilliant marketing director, called all of our customers before Channel 13 and the others broadcast the news around the region. She assured them that it was an accident, a tragic loss of one of our treasured employees, but it was not due to poor working conditions or mismanagement. She told them about our sterling safety record—tops in our industry.

Our customers trusted Genevieve so they pitied us and stuck with us, despite reducing their orders for tofu. No one could fault them for that—we're all practical business people.

Without Genevieve, I don't know how I'd have managed. Her warm and professional manner assured Becky's shocked factory friends the company would do its best to take care of Becky's family. She focused on how sad we all were, and made sure Becky's children were tended to by family and a minister.

I offered to call off production for the day, but the workers insisted on working. "Becky'd want us to." Even when I said it would be a paid day off, they persisted in wanting to work. Smart, down-to-earth folks. Keep the routine going to lessen their pain.

Gen managed Facebook with her usual brilliance and aplomb and tweeted all our followers with the news, condolences to the family, and notice of the foundation I told her we'd set up.

She set up a memorial page for Becky and her family with pictures and sympathetic comments from Becky's co-workers. She made a short video for Facebook of the company meeting I called, zooming in on the women's tears and the men's helpless expressions. Gen aimed the camera at my face, caught me sobbing, then quickly sobering up to show the staff how strong we all had to be.

Gen handled Twitter messages by posting empathetic notes and updates as any news came in. I referred the local media to her when I was finished answering their questions.

Before officially meeting with Chief Buhrman, I planned to give him the blue ribbon tour of the factory. At my office door his small hard hand gripped mine while he challenged me with his glassy brown eyes.

Buhrman was six inches shorter than me, trim and fit. He wore his navy blue uniform with padded shoulders. From the collar of his starched blue shirt to the cuffs of his pants, his outfit brooked no creases or lint. A polished brass badge jutted from his breast and a smaller badge rode just above the glossy brim of his hat.

Up close, decked out in full regalia, he reminded me of a Manhattan limo driver. But the fierce glare he shot at me from close-set eyes under beetled eyebrows warned me not to expect any servitude.

The herringboned mahogany butt of Buhrman's pistol bulged off his hip in a gleaming but aged and scarred black leather holster. Heightening the threat of the gun, he wore a shiny wide belt with a German Shepherd's narrow-eyed face embossed on the silver buckle.

A squalling cigarette pack-sized radio competed with a jangling ring of silver and brass keys to give his measured stride a clashing noise that reminded me of a school janitor's benign jingling as he pushed his broom.

*All bluff and bluster, but see his billy club? It's been used. Careful, buster.*

Trying to lighten up the encounter and gain a little power in this new relationship, I grinned. "We never had so much ordnance in our tofu factory before. We're mostly pacifists here."

He frowned and drew himself up.

"Just joking. Glad you're here."

He said, "We met before."

"I remember," I said.

"That Boys and Girls club fundraiser. You ran it, right?"

"Yeah. It was the YMCA."

Buhrman frowned.

"We raised almost a million dollars for the new therapy pool." I remembered how the guys at the Rotary Club joked how Buhrman insisted on being called "Chief."

The Chief nodded, pursing his lips.

"For the elderly. You know, lots of old folks get arthritis, need to work out in the water. It's easier on the bones." I wasn't getting through to him.

"Disabled kids, too. My kids are healthy but I felt getting that pool into town was a pretty important mission."

The Chief scratched his neck and said, "Yeah. My mother-in-law goes there every week. Does some kind of water acrobiotics." I grinned.

He stared into my eyes. "You know, we got us a pretty important mission right now, Mr. Greer."

Nodding, feeling that sinking feeling I get when things start to get out of control, I agreed. "We sure do. Gotta take care of that poor little family."

I noticed the Chief stood three feet from me, but his glare made it feel like he was about to crush against me.

Stretching a hairnet down over my ears and offering him one, I changed the subject, curbed his intrusion into my mindspace. I'd stick to my plan of impressing him with our professionalism and attention to details.

"Sanitation's our number one focus, Chief."

Buhrman grumbled "Food plant, it better be," and tugged the net down over his neatly parted brown hair.

We started with viewing the three forty-foot tall silos attached to our building where we stored up to three hundred thousand pounds of soybeans.

Inside the factory, we traced the route the beans followed as our machines processed them into tofu, past the soaking tanks where they found Becky, down the processing line to the cooking and the slurry area, to the extracting, where bean juice becomes 'soymilk.' We watched our state-of-the-art machinery change the soymilk into curds and whey.

"It's sort of like making cheese," I said. "We make curds and press them together into a soft cake."

He scowled. "Wouldn't catch me eating this stuff, especially not for dessert."

"It's not that kind of cake, Aaron." I laughed, always pleased to explain my unusual way of earning a living by making and selling a strange oriental food. "Some people do make pies and desserts out of it. We mostly eat it like meat—same way the Asian people do."

"Big place you got here, Charlie."

"Yeah. About an acre under one roof, with storage and offices." "Lotta places for somebody to hide."

*He's not here to grieve. Something up his sleeve.*

Waving off my suggestion that he wear earplugs, the Chief had also refused my offer of rubber boots. I in my galoshes, the Chief in his spit-polished, round-toed shoes, we sloshed through water that flowed half an inch deep across the production room floor.

Heavy soy-scented mist swirled around the cooking room and cold fog rose off the tanks where we iced down the finished tofu. The machine noise of bean grinding and the high-pressure steam-injection drowned out my words. Buhrman wasn't in a listening mood anyway. He moved slowly and stopped every few yards to observe.

"Did you notice the rows of panels on our roof?" I asked.

"Yeah. Solar. Must be tough to get enough sun this far north."

"You'd be surprised," I said. "We use it for hot water. Warms up the well water before it goes into the boiler. Energy efficiency. Saves money. Good for the future. I'm in this business for the good of society." I lowered my voice. "Want my kids and every kid to have a good future."

The Chief grunted, circled his finger in the air, motioned for us to carry on with our tour.

After circling past the chilling tanks and following the filled cases of tofu into the cooler, we stood on the loading dock watching a fork lift driver zip in and out of shipping trailers with pallets of tofu.

The Chief nodded his chin and flipped the hair net up in back, as if he finally understood something that had bothered him. "We'll get the photographers over. I want to see all your records, who came and went the other night."

'Getting the photographers over' meant hiring the only professional photographer in town away from his wedding and high school yearbook business. Later, when this thing blew over, maybe we could use some of the shots in our brochures or the web site.

*You better get real, or Buhrman will bury American Tofu. How will if feel when you go down, too?*

"Sure thing," I said. "We'll check the time clock records. Would you like to speak with the workers?" It made sense to take a cooperative stance. In my business dealings, I practiced win-win negotiation, and the Chief clearly had to win something here.

He said, "You bet. I hope they speak English."

"We have translators. Spanish, Chinese, Vietnamese. Our Cambodian workers speak English."

"Good. I need to talk with everybody."

"We've always had an international crew, the way it is nowadays. Globalism, you know."

"Yeah. That's smart. Get 'em cheap. Illegals, too, I bet."

"No illegals here, Aaron." I smiled. "When I started the company, we had Zen monks working here. Best workers I ever had."

Buhrman furrowed his brows. "You got monkeys working here?"

"No, no," I laughed. "Monks, Aaron. Not monkeys. Zen's a Japanese religion. Monks. Tofu is a big industry in Japan."

"Monks? Oh, yeah, like priests. Ever heard of 'anchorites'? Monks who live in the desert."

'Anchorites?' He was a Bible reader.

"I'm Catholic myself," he said. "We have monks, y'know. Call 'em Trappists. Famous for their jams and honey and things. The wife's on a kick lately, spreads blueberry jam from the monastery on my Sunday pancakes. Ever try that?"

"Sounds tasty."

"After Mass, with a cuppa joe? Mmm." Ambling along the loading dock like old friends talking, Buhrman stopped in the shadow at the corner of the building and squinted up at me and said, "What was that you said? Japs?"

"Yes. Japanese."

"Thought so."

"Japanese taught us how to make tofu. They've made it for centuries in shops and factories. To them it's like milk or cheese. Big business over there. Tofu is like their dairy industry."

Buhrman challenged me again. "I always thought Japs looked like monkeys. Little squirts hopping around in swarms, squeaking, taking pictures. Best thing Harry Truman ever did. I've seen all the Hiroshima clips on the History Channel. Too bad they're black and white."

He was feeding me, testing my politics, testing my will with his belligerence. He'd gone right at the core of my belief that we have to open up to every culture if we're going to save the human race from itself. Amicable as any Chamber of Commerce member talking to the town's only security force, I grinned and said, "You mean The Bomb."

"That's it. The Big One."

Shaking my head, I wondered how to adapt my progressive attitudes to this racist yokel. I had to take his guff, no matter what, stay on his side. If I upset him, he might want to make an example of me. Still, I had to appear spontaneous and natural. He'd made it clear that he expected me to be at least a little odd.

He turned away and examined the cars and pickups in the parking lot, then turned deliberately. "Anything else you wanna show me, Charlie?"

"That's about it."

"What's out back?" he asked.

"Oh, I forgot. Didn't think it could have anything to do with the accident."

"You never know."

Outside, the temperature had already climbed to the high seventies and the oaks that circled the industrial park showed early scars of tans among their deep green leaves.

Sun-glistened corn stalks ripened in the nearby fields waiting for the combines to strip and chop them into silage for the county's abundant cattle.

Since cooperation was my only strategy until he revealed his intentions, I guided him toward the rear of the factory. "Beautiful day. Indian summer's early this year. Hope it stays like this for the funeral."

"Never a nice day for a young person's funeral." The Chief sounded angry.

"Yeah. It was sad. Horrible for the kids. We're doing everything we can for the family but, you know, we gotta keep the business moving if we're gonna help anybody. It's really sad," I said, unable to stop my voice from wavering.

*Greer, he's a snoop. Don't show him your feelings. He's not your dupe.*

I'm not his dupe, either.

At the rail line behind the plant, six black open-topped rail cars hunkered in a line, waiting to be filled with ground-up soy pulp.

"When I look at these rail cars, they seem like hogs the size of dinosaurs queuing up for feed," I said.

Buhrman grunted.

Beyond the tracks, our five-acre sludge pond filtered the gray water before sending it into the town's sewage disposal system.

"We call it the 'Blue Lagoon,'" I said, my voice firm again. He didn't get the joking old movie reference.

"See those rail cars, Aaron? They're one of my biggest profit centers. See that stainless steel pipe coming out of the side of the building and the yellowish stuff dropping out? That's *okara*, ground soy pulp, the waste from production."

He squatted and picked up a moist clump and sniffed it.

I said, "Crushed soybeans with the soymilk removed. We fill the cars with okara and send them to a ConAgra hog farm a couple of hours downstate. They empty the cars and we get a nice price for it. The profit from okara pays employee Christmas bonuses."

We watched the okara drizzle out of the pipe and disappear like wet tan snow into the rail car.

"Smart, Greer," he said. "Waste not, want not."

Squeezing the clump of soy pulp between his thumb and fingers, Buhrman said, "I always thought soybeans were animal food. My cousin feeds his hogs and cattle soy and corn."

"Yeah, well, the factory hog farm mixes the okara with corn and vitamins and antibiotics, anything else hogs need. Once the okara leaves here, no human touches it again before the hogs chow down. Feed's all mixed together underground and conveyed to the hogs on a continuous belt. It's an infinite swill trough. They call it 'Hog Heaven.'"

Buhrman shook his head. "Never knew where your bacon comes from."

"I thought about investing in hogs, I said. "You only need one man to supervise two thousand hogs. The least labor intensive manufacturing business you can imagine."

The Chief turned away from the rail line and started back toward the front of the factory. "To each his own. I'm not really much interested in livestock. I like my animals in the wild, like deer. You hunt, Charlie?"

"When I was a kid. Not since."

"Been shooting since I was five. Always loved it. Those gun control idiots in Washington never had the pleasure of eating meat they spent all day tracking in the freezing woods." Buhrman raised his hand to his nose and jerked his head, indicating the rear of the plant. "Stinks back there."

"Yeah. Okara decays fast, especially in warm weather.

He raised his eyebrows and wrinkled his forehead. "Like this case. The longer it sits around, the rottener it smells."

***

After walking the loop around the property line, we returned to my office to have our real talk.

"Good tour, Charlie," he said. "I always wondered what went on up here. But, goddam it, my feet're soaked."

Instead of reminding him that he'd refused the boots, I tossed him the towel and a pair of thick cotton socks from my travel kit in the closet. He dried between his toes and pulled on the socks. We wiped off his soggy shoes and flicked drops off the glossy toes with the towel.

"You know I don't want to cause you any trouble," he said bending over his laces.

My heart sank.

"We found some strange things. I have to come up with answers," he said, tying equal and precisely balanced bows that stood out perpendicular to the sides of the shoes. Sitting up and staring at me with his bulging eyes, he said, "I never investigated a murder before."

"Murder!" I said. "Who says it's murder?" Panic lanced my stomach. My thighs clenched and I had to grip the chair to stop myself from leaping up and bouncing around the room.

"Nobody—yet. Some things about the body don't add up to just a little accident."

"Like what?" I said, breathing deep to stifle my fear. Employing one of my sales techniques, I tried to act like his co-investigator so he'd feel I was on his side.

"Cause of death. Bludgeon by a blunt instrument. Coulda drove a chunk of skull right into her brain. As it was, she hemorrhaged."

I thought a minute and said, avoiding the mistake of defensiveness, "That's news. We thought she drowned."

Buhrman grunted. "Not only that. Her stomach was full of tofu. I mean, crammed full. Like someone shoveled it down her throat. Mixed with alcohol, beef, nuts. Big appetite for a little lady."

"Oh," I chuckled, "the tofu in her stomach, that's easy. The first shift sautés up a batch of scrambled tofu. It looks and tastes like scrambled eggs. No cholesterol, though. Did you ever try it?"

I gush about my favorite subjects when I'm nervous, but I caught myself and snapped back to my objective executive posture. "Most of our people take advantage of our free tofu breakfast policy. She probably ate some. Or else she had it at her party the night before." "No way I'll ever try that. I like my eggs real, over easy. Cholesterol doesn't worry me. Not like murder."

Buhrman's melodrama pissed me off. "Aaron, this is not *CSI Miami*. You're looking into small town, small factory industrial accident. I want to help you as much as I can. Please. Don't act like some uptight city cop. We can figure this out. You have my total support."

My tough CEO side, the serious businessman who could see through everybody's act, permitted no silliness. At the same time, he had to see that I was a solid citizen, thoroughly behind the efforts of our town's diligent timvestigator: him. All the time my nerves tingled and the muscles in my legs twitched.

"Relax, Charlie. So she had too much tofu for breakfast. I hear the stuff gives you gas. Do you think her own farts made her dizzy and she fell on her face?" Buhrman cackled.

Stone-faced, gritting my teeth, I thought, what do you expect from the police in a town named Clement? "Chief, if you don't have anything more serious ... How can I help you now?"

Burhman's eyes darted around the room, taking in the details. He'd never been anywhere decorated with so many exotic statues and fabrics and souvenirs.

*He thinks you're weird. Makes him suspicious. You better act calm, normal, and gracious.*

"Do I need to call my lawyer?"

"No. Take it easy." He smiled and leaned back, extending his legs and fiddling with a souvenir teacup from my stay in the Miyamasi Hotel in Tokyo. "Just looking for ideas here. We have to examine at every angle. We found a high level of THC and alcohol in her blood. No Ecstasy or crystal meth. I suspected that when I first heard about the death, but no."

I didn't want to discuss drugs, unless I could discover how important they were in his assessment of Becky's death. I knew we had a problem, especially with the immigrant workers and the part-time high school kids, but Becky had told me she never got involved with it. "Yeah. We're all for abstinence," I said.

Buhrman raised his eyebrows.

"Drugs, I mean." He nodded and relaxed his face. "We make our annual donation to the police department's Drug & Alcohol Prevention program. Gotta keep the kids sober. You cops do the best job you can."

He coughed. "Keep everybody sober. Keep your money coming, Charlie. Between you and me? Fighting drugs is a losing battle." "What?"

"Keeps two men I need on the payroll is why the government keeps the program in town. Still, if it stops one kid from getting hooked, it's worth it."

Everyone knew that about Clement's D&AP, but the Chief's disclosure to a business taxpayer about its futility sounded like negotiation. An honest man who wasn't afraid to reveal personal opinions different from the usual ones expected revelations about my reality. That made him a dangerous man to lead an investigation that was bound to implicate me, if he got some breaks. I'd have to get to his supervisor somehow. I gave Bill Murphy on the town council a decent contribution last election. He might help.

Taking the lead, I moved our talk back to Becky. "Scuttlebutt here says she was probably still high from her birthday when she came to work. Drugs and alcohol: main cause of industrial accidents."

"Yeah. If it was an accident."

"Anything else in her blood?"

"Like what?"

I risked self-exposure. "HIV, or something?"

He sat back. "Why?"

"I don't know. Maybe clues about the kind of life she lived?" "What do you want us to do? Check everybody who has HIV in the state and see if she slept with them? But good point. Any lovers of hers are suspect. Do you know who she was, uh, going out with?" I kept my face blank, unblinking.

"Y'know, illicit relations. Screwing." He looked away when he said "screwing" as if embarrassed.

"No idea." I wasn't really worried about HIV because I'd always used a condom, but you never know if you can get it from kissing. I never thought about it when I was with her, our whole affair felt so natural and wholesome—a calling from the goddess of love that nothing bad could touch.

*That goddess of love is one scary dame. Lets you feel divine, then drops you into a tank of shame.*

Now came my chance to find out what Buhrman knew, if anything, about her and me. The question could backfire. "Did you find anything at her house that gave you any clues?"

He didn't answer for a long minute, his cheeks flat and his eyes cold as he held mine.

"Charlie, I know you're used to being the boss, but this is my investigation. You can help by keeping your nose out of it unless I ask you something."

"Hold it, Aaron. I'm trying to help here." I waited for him to speak but we sat staring at each other for an uncomfortable silent minute so I changed the subject back to drugs. "As long as my workers come to work and produce, I never wanted them to have those mandatory urine tests. Maybe I should start."

"Yeah. They all smoke and drink. We know it. You don't have to test for that. I'm sure you watch out for speed these days. What worries me is the bump on her head. Big as my thumb. Like someone clubbed her."

"Most likely she fell and banged her head on the tank," I said. "They lift sixty pound bushel bags of beans and carry them up the ladder. It's kind of a steep ladder. She lost her balance and slipped."

"Could be." He paused. "It's, well, we have some problems."

I waited.

"Coroner says the woman had been dead at least two hours before they found her."

I'd thought about that and had my answer ready, but held back. Speaking slowly in a puzzled tone, I said "Day crew gets started between two and three. She was the first one on the schedule. She could have come in at two, and been dead in ten minutes. They found her at what? Four?"

"Give or take." He stared at me. "What about her wet clothes." "Wet clothes? You'd have wet clothes if you were lay-ing in a tank of beans that soaked all night in water."

"This is no joke. I mean the clothes in her locker. Had some moss on the seat of her shorts. Mud. Pieces of leaves in the elas-tic. Twigs."

"Mmm," I mumbled as if considering what he might think it meant. "Must have sat on the ground at her party?"

"Hey, good idea, Charlie. They told me you were sharp. I'll check it out."

Who told him that? I let it go. "Pretty thorough investiga-tion." "Background. You know. Gotta have something to go on before the D. A. gives me the full steam go-ahead. Warrants and such."

District Attorney? This was serious. Buhrman was the type of cop who'd love grandstanding to his higher-ups whether he had anything substantial or not.

Leaning forward and resting his elbows on his knees, Buhrman propped his jaw on thumbs. Speaking through folded fingers, he said , "You know what's got me stumped? Maybe you have another idea here."

I waited for what felt like a full minute. Losing patience, I almost said, You should try out for the new reality TV show. *Big Chiefs*. You have the flair.

He said, "I wonder where she got the skin we found under her fingernails."

"God." I got up. I pace when I'm thinking something out, walk in tight circles if I'm in the office, take a few trips around the neighborhood if I have to think really hard. Buhrman watched me with a thin smile on his face.

"What skin? When did you find that?"

"We had it all along. We'll wait till after the funeral. Respect for the family, it's how we handle this type of thing in Clement. Hold off the formal investigation so people can mourn and have their services without the commotion of a murder."

Besides, I thought, he needed the time to get his ducks in a row. I sensed he was propping me up in his shooting gallery, the big mallard drake whose iridescent green neck begged for the bullet.

"Charlie, this may not be *CSI Miami* but we got the same kinda problems. Y'know, once we find the motive? We're good as found the killer."

"We don't know if it's a murder." He couldn't bully me.

"Explain this." He leaned forward and jutted out his lower lip while he spoke. "She was dead at least two hours. Somebody could have killed her, then dumped her body in the factory. That wasn't soybeans under her nails, unless you tell me your beans bleed."

"Sure," I said, chuckling, trying to lighten him up. "We make 'em bleed. Soymilk, not blood."

"Yeah, well, we gotta check everyone's bodies here. See who's got any strange scratches before they heal. Anybody's got scratches, we'll do a DNA test real quick. Lab downstate handles this kind of thing. Top priority." He studied me through narrowed, triumphant eyes.

"If she didn't try to fight off her killer, scratch the hell out of him, I'll bet my badge! We'll know everything in two, three weeks."

*Buhrman found something to make his career. Just make sure it ain't you, Greer.*

He was in his late thirties and he obviously thought himself capable of far more than supervising little Clement's Saturday night drunk driving traps and domestic abuse patrols. Just being involved in a murder investigation would sharpen up his résumé and if this happened to be a crime and he happened to solve it, his future was secure. He could go anywhere in the state.

I had to use every ounce of sales skill I'd developed over the years to keep Buhrman under control. "Aaron," I said, casually sitting down beside him, "do you know what you're getting into here? This town has eighty-three jobs riding on American Tofu. Eighty-three jobs that weren't here a few years ago. I'm proud of those jobs."

He nodded and licked his lips.

"Didn't we help your niece out when she got pregnant? Now she's in college! A lot of people start out working in the factory here. We move them up fast as we can." I paused, letting him think, then continued. "I'm glad to help. We both want the same thing. If we have a murderer out there, let's get him. But all you have is a theory. For God's sake, let's keep it calm and quiet until we have something we can prove."

He edged away from me. "No problem, Charlie. It's to all our benefits. But don't bring my family up—"

"It's all our families—"

"It's not about families. It's about murder." His face reddened and he stood up. "Maybe your family's next!" Striding across the office, he stumbled on a crease in the rug I'd brought back from Istanbul.

"You think I'm having fun here? You may be playing around with your barrel of monkeys up here in Tofuland, but you know what? There's plenty of folks in town—taxpayers on the town council who wouldn't mind if your tofu business left Clement." Contempt tinged his voice. "They wouldn't have to pay for the new sewage plant to take care of all the crap you flush out of your slush pond."

"Sludge pond, Aaron. Lagoon! Blue Lagoon." The news about the town council surprised me, though I had a pretty good idea that the council needed someone to blame for the property tax increase they just voted in this year. Not only that, Buhrman probably wanted to buy a new patrol car and the council told him he had to wait.

"So, let me ask you this," Buhrman went on, a tight smile cutting his face. "Will you be the first to let us inspect your skin? I already cleared time with Doc Wallace at the clinic. Whad'ya say?"

"Sure," I fumbled.

Becky scratched me the last time we made love. I remember yelping and jerking as she dug her fingernails into my shoulders.

Sometimes, she played a little rough, growling and biting me and she liked me to pinch her nipples hard. When we first started sleeping together, I had to tell her to back off with the nails on my ass and back. I didn't want marks on my body in case Nora might notice them.

After that, when she started to scratch, she'd ask me if it hurt. But the night before she died, she was wilder than ever. Could traces of my skin have stuck under her nails? If they did, no matter what I'd done to cover my trail, I didn't have a chance.

The Chief shifted in his chair and said, "Well? It won't take long."

As I considered what to tell him, my eyebrows lifted and my shoulders shrugged in innocence. I had to be imagining it but Becky's scratch burned across my shoulder hot as a brand. It should have faded by now. I'd have to check it in the mirror.

Everybody knows a guilty mind can cause physical symptoms and guilt was not on my mental agenda. It was love and if you have to feel guilty about love, you might as well give up your citizenship.

Still, if the doctor mentioned the scratch to the Chief, my reaction would be embarrassment. Nora hadn't touched me all summer, but if the Chief asked me about it, I'd tell him to leave my bedroom out of this.

Stalling, for no good reason, I said, "Why me, Aaron. I was home in bed. Ask my wife."

"Sorry, Charlie. You're the big cheese. Oh, excuse me," he said with a sarcastic downturn to his lips, "the big tofu. You volunteer and everyone else follows. The best motive we've come up with is jealousy or her boyfriend beating her up. Happens all the time."

He was right. That's usually the case.

"We don't know who she was sleeping with yet. Maybe he was trying to shut her up about something. Who knows? I can think of half a dozen reasons. We're checking everybody."

I stood up and walked toward the door, eager to end the interview. "No problem. I'll head over. Have my secretary tell everybody they can get half an hour's pay."

"You don't have to do that."

"Least I can do."

"All right. It's your money." He stopped at the door. "I have to say, Charlie, you were so fired up by this, you're making me wonder a little bit. A man who runs a company and wears a diamond earring and has a cube of tofu tattooed on is arm is just a little bit peculiar and worth checking out, don't you think?"

He smiled as if he were teasing me the way your best friend would kid you when he knew you were fibbing.

I couldn't tell whether Buhrman wanted to intimidate me or not but I already knew he was not the kind of man who joked around. Coming after his sinister comment about dropping the atomic bomb on Japan, his remark about my earring didn't faze me. A Clement, New York, police chief would define conservative in any dictionary.

"What's that scratch on your chin, Charlie? About three days old?" The smile stayed on his face, but his eyes squinted with real interest.

My hand shot to my face to feel the inch-long scab that grew on the underside of my chin.

"Playing with my kids." I spoke too quickly, as if I'd prepared, and I had.

Stammering, I went on, "What? You really think I had something to do with it?" I modulated my outrage, not wanting to alienate him, but making sure he knew he was out of bounds.

"Naw, not yet, anyway. Still, I'm not sure you were nowhere near the factory that night? I heard you work late sometimes, real late."

"Don't mess with me, Aaron. You want a successful business, you work all hours of the day and night."

He smiled again, without sarcasm or any kind of pleasure. "I'm not 'messing up' anybody. It's Investigation 101 here: Everybody who had anything to do with MacDaniel better have a good alibi."

"In that case: I didn't work late that night. Check with my wife. Sound asleep, same bed."

"I'm gonna. Don't worry. We gotta start somewhere. See where she was at that night."

"I told you. Why are you being so aggressive, Aaron?" I raised my voice. "Because my wife and I own the company and you think we're to blame for an accident?"

"Take it easy. All in the day's work. Besides, there's rumors around town about you and women."

"Ridiculous. Rumors don't get far in court. I bet there are plenty of rumors about you and women, too. Any man who's anybody in a small town like this gets gossiped about."

He glared at me and I saw the mistake I made, giving him an opening to distance himself.

"Don't worry, Chief," I said, cooling off my pique and playing it safe, giving his ego the respect it needed to render me a somewhat neutral character in the murder drama he was concocting. "I'll head over to Doc Wallace's right away. I have nothing to hide."

"I'm afraid I have to ask you to get all your employees over to the clinic, right away. It's already been three days too many. We gotta check everybody before their scabs heal up. By the way," he said, flipping his Chief's hat onto his head, his eyes glittering. He tossed out his trump. "Did you know she was pregnant?"

"What?"

"Yeah. Two, three months. Now we have a double murder."

"Double murder?"

"Two people died, that's double. One adult. One child. That's how we think in Clement, anyhow. It's New York law."

*Double your trouble. Double his fun.*

I stared at him, my stomach rumbling and my lungs beginning to wheeze.

"One more thing. From now on, I gotta ask you to let me know when you or your people go out of town."

"What? Are we all suspects? You don't have any evidence this is anything more than an accident. Somebody's always on the road. I can't be calling you and asking permission to run my business."

"Well, just for courtesy's sake."

"What do you mean?"

"Work with me on this. That's all."

"All right. Aaron," I said, "in the spirit of getting this behind us. I already told you I'd work with you. But you should know I'm leaving the country for a couple of weeks."

"Leaving the country? I don't know. How long you had this planned?"

"Since June. Relax, Aaron. I'm going to Taiwan—business."

"Oh. You go overseas a lot?"

"Not really. This is a big trip. Bought my Taipei tickets last spring."

Buhrman's eyebrows lifted slightly as if he was thinking, 'Hey, maybe Greer set something up here.'

*Don't protest. He could guess the rest.*

My Jiminy Cricket voice was right. My view of Buhrman's abilities as an interviewer, and my apprehension, climbed inch by inch up my own alertness monitor.

Finally, he said, "Leave me your Taipei number in case I need you."

"I was planning on it. I hope you'll keep me informed of anything you find."

"You'll hear plenty. You know, I never went to China. Wife and I went to Rome a few years ago with the NYCPA. Catholic Policemen's Association? Beautiful city. Loved every minute. Know what I remember best?"

I breathed easier. "Never been there. What?"

"The catacombs."

I shook my head and smiled. "Bones," I said. "You liked the bones."

"You know why? Because that's what it's all about. This life is a bone yard and we're all cemetery keepers."

"That's depressing."

"Maybe. But think about it. I do."

"Yeah, you're right. We all end up the same place but I don't think about it much." He waited and I changed the subject back to our mutual interest. "I'm glad to help however I can," I said. "Let's get this thing done and move on."

He perked up. "Great. One little thing you can do? I'm going to send someone over to pick up copies of your personnel records for the last couple of years. Everybody's file, payroll, that stuff."

"You better get a legal order. Employment files are private and confidential."

"I'll do what I have to do."

I nodded.

"Last thing. We might need other records. Email, bonuses, profits, taxes. That kind of thing."

"You'll definitely need a subpoena or warrant or something. I'm not giving you my private business information just to satisfy your curiosity. Call Harold Fierst at his office if you want to talk to him about anything legal."

"Yeah, well. I'll wait on that. If I need anything, I'm sure Judge Kreppel will pave the way. Meantime, round up your troops and send them over to Wallace. We gotta see who the victim scratched." He grinned at me, his eyes sparkling with excitement. "I'll have a man over at Wallace's. He'll take everybody's prints."

"Prints? Fingerprints?"

Buhrman nodded and pursed his lips.

"Is it legal?"

"Of course. Easier that way. Get all the nuts 'n bolts outta the way in one place."

***

After the Chief left, I walked down the semi-rural street in front of the factory. Locusts were sawing at the old oaks and the air dripped with summer's best effort at dissolving everything into soggy sponges.

I had no idea Becky was pregnant. Did she know she was knocked up before she seduced me that night? If she did, she was playing me for a sucker ... but I don't think so. For one thing, she was too honest, too real with me to hide something like that. She always wanted to use a rubber. That couldn't have been an act, but wouldn't I have seen her body morphing, her breasts and nipples getting bigger, maybe some belly showing.

It's not like I haven't had two kids myself and seen exactly how a woman's body changes. Becky's baby wasn't mine. But what if one of the rubbers had split and we didn't notice. If it did and that baby's mine, I'm screwed.

*You're a business guy with skin in the game. You didn't use a skin and it's gonna prove your blame.*

That skin under Becky's nails? She had to have washed a dozen times since we made love, done dishes, soaked her fingers while she was at work the day she died. For that matter, while she lay in the tank that night, her hands were under the wet beans a foot below the surface. It was amazing that after all that, Buhrman found something stuck under them.

If it was somebody else's skin—who else? I started wondering if she was fooling around with somebody besides me. No, not possible. Could have been food or dirt—she liked to garden. Maybe playing frisbee or volleyball at her party.

I worried most about the DNA test, but that was only one of Buhrman's attack plans. He would pry into every aspect of my life and my family's and everybody's in the company. I'd stonewall if he had a legitimate idea or lead and if not, I'd continue to cooperate, to keep him off balance.

His threats about forcing me to supply confidential company information gave me a good idea. I went back to the office and called Adam.

Adam had computerized the company a few years back when I hired him as an intern from RPI . He did so much for us that whenever we needed computer help, we brought him in.

The one person you have to trust in business is your computer guy. I trusted Adam. He'd taught me everything I knew about computers and I'd taught him a few things about business. The basic policy we conducted our relationship on was discretion, at all times. What went on between him and me and the computers nobody needed to know, but us, and neither of us asked why.

I asked Adam to meet me at the Wendy's across from Doc Wallace's clinic. I was sure he could teach me to route copies of everybody's internet and intranet emails, searches, downloads, and anything else to my home computer. The last thing I could afford to do with my time was to spy on my employees, but right then, I had to prepare for anything and everything. If I didn't, Charlie Greer and American Tofu could be history. The kind of history you want to forget and can't: the bloody kind.

# Chapter Four

## *Genevieve O'Connor*

# GEN'S FIVE MEN AND A FUNERAL

Charlie called me at six in the morning the day they found Becky MacDaniel floating in the soybean soaking vat. He mumbled something like he thought it was me and thank God it wasn't but now we had to take care of business. He rambled on until he said, "Call Nora at home. She'll tell you what happened. I'll call you in an hour. We got a lot of work to do today. Thank you, Genevieve. Stay alive. Don't do anything stupid."

What was he was talking about? Becky MacDaniel was a plant worker who I knew slightly. She had a couple of kids in my son Liam's school, and I felt immediately how terrible her death would be to them. The only worse thing than losing your child is losing your parent as a kid. I know. I lost my mother when I was ten.

Nora told me the story of how the morning start-up crew found the body. "Damn Benko," she said. "He called to tell us and first he said it was you. Then we found out it was that poor woman Becky. She must have slipped and hit her head on the tank."

"I barely knew her."

"I half-remember her from the company picnic, but ... what a horrible way to die." Her voice trembled.

"Don't think about it."

"We have to talk." Nora's voice trembled. "Do something for the family, not just flowers. She had two kids. Single mom, y'know."

"Relax, Nora. I'm taking care of it. Meantime, help Charlie relax. He's freaked."

"Like if I wasn't?" she said. "We never dealt with anything like this before."

Before he left for school I told my son, Liam, what happened. "A lot of your friends have parents who work at American Tofu. They'll be upset about the accident."

"Good thing you don't work in the factory," Liam said, two tiny wrinkles crossing his twelve-year old forehead.

"The office is safe, safest place in town, sweetie. People will be talking at school, but don't worry. Call me if you need to, otherwise, we'll talk when I get home. Maybe we'll go out for pizza."

"It's not Friday," he said, protecting our ritual week-ending meal at the Monster Pizza Patch.

"O.K., honey. How about Dori's Dairy Diner?"

"Good idea. I'm gonna have their Fatty Fat Burger."

"No fries if you order that."

"C'mon, Mom. I need the calories for swim team. See you tonight." He gave me a quick hug and ran out the door.

I watched him ride his bike up the street, dreading what I was sure to face in the office: Charlie frazzled, Benko wondering what to do, frightened factory workers, calculating customers whose confidence in us I had to maintain. All the bad publicity could wreck all the work I did to make the company as successful as it is.

Plenty of problems had come my way in the last couple of years, but this one burned in my stomach. We were too close to being totally out of control.

***

At work by eight, I braced for the grueling job of fielding calls from the media and explaining to customers what happened. Almost before I sat down, Benko stepped into my office and locked the door behind him.

"Did you hear?" he said.

"Of course. Charlie called me at six. What do you think I've been doing since then?"

He sighed. "Yeah."

"Charlie told me you found her."

His eyes flashed. "Chen did. I called cops, ran here, called Charlie. I was sound sleeping."

He reeked of sweat and his breath stank of garlic and booze. The odor of his musky sweat usually excited me, but that morning it was sour.

Benko was the handsomest men I'd ever met. Two inches taller than my five eleven, he wore his thick ash-blond hair in a long crew cut. The straight hair flopped sideways on his head, giving his lined face an odd boyish look, a hurt but brave boy. Thin, somewhat narrow shoulders, but enormous hands hung off muscular arms like paws. Long wide fingers sprouted from broad meaty palms. Somewhere in his forties, he probably had a dozen years on my thirty two.

The first time I saw Benko, he gripped a large pipe wrench like a baton. Pale and hairless, the back of his hand was boldly sculpted with bulging veins risen like blue ridges crossing his thick wrist. I watched the hands maneuver the wrench around motors and pumps in the factory, tightening bolts, loosening buckles, testing joints, the heavy wrench slow-dancing with the steel machinery

He spotted me watching, then smiled the warmest, openest smile. "You like my tool?" He waggled the wrench like a magic wand. "Monkey wrench. Makes loose and tight any nut you got." I smiled at his crude flirtation and waved without replying and walked on to pick up tofu samples from the cooler, wondering if his eyes were brown or blue.

I found out a few days later when I stopped in the factory at six o'clock one morning to organize my day's sales presentations. We met in the company kitchen. In a gruff voice, Benko introduced himself

He said he knew who I was and he understood I was the most important person in the company, " ... because, we learned in Russia from Americans. Only with sale, business starts."

Of course, when anyone reminded me that all my hard work meant something besides my rent check and Liam's new shoes, my ego cheered. Now, Benko gave me more than appreciation for my sales work.

Nobody else knew about our late-night dates and I intended to keep it that way. And I didn't like talking to him behind a closed and locked door—too many curious eyes and flapping mouths in the office, even in the emergency of Becky's death. When I reached for the door handle to unlock and open it, he clenched my wrist.

"Ow." I knocked his hand away. "What's the matter with you?"

"Not yet. Lock for now."

"Why?

"Will they come after me?" Benko's eyes narrowed and his fleshy lips pursed. "They will, I know."

Letting the doorknob go I turned to him, putting my hands on his shoulders. "Sit down, Benko. Relax. Why would they come after you? Becky tripped and fell. Charlie thinks she was probably still drunk from last night. Her birthday party. Everyone knows she's a party girl."

He shuddered. "I was there with her, celebrating. They find out and blame me. I gave her Azteca. Expensive tequila. Big bottle. They find some way to lock me in."

"Wait a minute, Benko. This isn't the old days in Russia. We still don't lock people up because they went to a party with someone who accidentally died."

He slumped into a chair, shaking his head. I went to him and held him, caressing his damp forehead

"Baby, take it easy. I'll cover for you. Nobody can come after you just because you're a foreigner. Half the plant is immigrants."

"You wait," he growled and reached around me and pulled my belly to his cheek

His unexpected fear softened my heart as I rubbed his steel-cable shoulders. "Let's go to dinner tonight, just us," I said. "It's good if people see us together now. Colleagues."

He perked up. "You come over after?"

"We'll see," I winked.

He stood at the door, his eyes narrowed and his jaw set. He turned to leave and opened the door, then looked back.

"I got bad feelings. Real bad."

I waited.

"About Charlie."

My mouth dropped. "What?"

"He's in this somehow."

"What? Impossible."

"Don't know, Gen. What you call it, 'Gut pain?'" His hand circled his abdomen. "Down here something I know."

Benko stepped into the hall and stood still. His head and shoulders sagged forward and his long arms hung down nearly to his knees, his prehensile fingers curling. For a moment I thought he might drop to the carpet and keen.

He poised himself, bouncing on his toes. His back to me, he raised his head, jutting his chin, and hulked down the hall, his arms swinging front to back.

I watched him go then closed and locked the door, and went to work.

✳✳✳

Charlie had hired Benko Gladonov a few months before Becky died. He said that Benko needed a chance to expand his good work record in the States, and he'd worked in a food company overseas as well as in Albany.

"Immigrants usually work for reasonable pay," Charlie told the staff during a management meeting. "We help them launch themselves into the mainstream. It's a win-win." Charlie's altruism always included a business arrangement favorable to him.

That summer I found myself spending several pleasant, diverting evenings with Benko. We walked around the sidewalks of my neighborhood or sat on my porch swing and talked about tofu and business and he told me his life story.

As a suspected Jew in Russia, he endured beatings and ostracism. Benko laughed when he said, "It should be easy. I pull my pants down and show my natural thing, but my father was hygiene man. Expert, so he had me cut." Benko grew up the child of the manager of a large dairy commune so he knew farms and milk processing as his second nature, but, "My heart," he thumped himself on the chest, "is true Russian: heart of rebel, not farmer.

Because he didn't perform to his father's or the commune's standards, he was expelled and joined the army. A fistfight with an officer in the army landed him in prison for six months and kept him out of Afghanistan. He spent his twenties on the streets of Moscow begging and stealing and running errands for whoever would pay him anything, tempted to join a gang

Before glasnost made wealthy entrepreneurs of his criminal cohorts, Benko had fled to London where he parlayed his early experience on the farm into a job in a mincemeat pie factory. He got married and had two children before he divorced

"Should have joined gang in Moscow," he mused one night as we rocked on my porch swing. "I'd be rich man now. Boss. I miss my Brit babies. All time, I think how I fly them to Daddy."

"Why don't you?"

"Mother. Brit bitch. She has court papers. Me? They put me in jail I try to see my babies."

I let the subject of his children slide because I wasn't ready to get serious with any man. Still, Benko's eagerness to be with me was flattering. He acted like an adoring teenager trying to impress a favorite teacher he has a crush on, and I was at least ten years younger than he.

"Those puppy-dog eyes are almost irresistible, Benko. Is that how men flirt in Russia?"

"I never flirt," he said. "In Russia, you feel something, you don't do flirt."

"Here you flirt to have fun. It doesn't mean anything."

"You teach me to flirt," he winked.

"That's good," I grinned and winked back.

I always maintained a policy of no personal involvement with my fellow employees, and I made that clear to Benko the first time we had dinner. He said he agreed with me totally

"Except," he said, "in Russia, passion rules principles. But, this is America. You're my boss, Genevieve. Whatever you say, I will do."

He glanced away then looked up and held my stare. If I wanted him, he was mine.

Benko growled "Genevieve." Four syllables rumbling directly out of his chest siezed my name like one of his wrenches, turning it between his tongue and teeth as if it were a piece of soft metal. Soon enough, we all learned that Benko was a master of torque.

***

I had to call Gianni Giordano, my best customer and my ex-lover. Since we'd broken up a year ago, I'd avoided him, until now.

He still wanted to sleep with me and we were still best friends, as far as he was concerned. From his traditional Italian male position as the head of a long line of patriarchs and successful businessmen, he saw no reason we shouldn't be lovers. I fell for him as hard as he fell for me, but a mistress role with him or anyone was out of the question.

I told his secretary it was an emergency. Gianni didn't need to work, but he showed up every day by dawn at his produce business as he had for twenty-five years.

"Hello, beautiful," he said. "Wait a minute. I have to get off the other line. It's the Pope, but he can call back."

I laughed and held the line.

Nervous but excited to hear his voice, when he came back on the line, I said, "Let's do FaceTime."

In a few seconds, his gorgeous face bloomed onto the phone. He was tanner than usual, and his smile melted my heart. He beamed and waved, mouthing a kiss. My stomach flipped.

"Gianni, I have some bad news."

He sat up. I could only see his chin for a minute.

"Are you all right? What can I do?"

"I'm fine. It's not me. It's about American Tofu."

"It can't be that bad."

"Somebody died. A woman. One of our workers died in the factory."

"I'm sorry." He fell silent. I knew he was considering how the death could affect his business. "Unfortunately people die in factories all the time."

"She had kids, a boy and a girl. Liam knows them."

"I'll send something for the funeral. What about a fund for the kids?"

"We just heard about the death. We haven't thought about anything." Except holding back chaos.

"Charlie?"

"He's a mess."

"Tell him to relax. This happens all the time. I lost a man to a fork lift ... years ago, but ... It's a war wound—if you have employees, sometimes you lose them. It happens to everybody in this business. Where are you?"

"In the office."

"Call me later. If you run into anybody who gives you trouble, tell them American Tofu has one hundred percent support from Giordano. Tell them whatever Genevieve says, it's the truth and that's all there is to it."

"Thanks. That'll help." I would do anything for him, except sleep with him now.

"Good luck. Call whenever. I miss you. I want to see you."

"Maybe when the uproar is over. I'll be in New York sometime in the next couple of months. How about having lunch?"

"That's the best invitation I've had since the last time you took me out."

"Stop it, Gianni." We both laughed. "Right now I have to concentrate on work."

"It's all right," he said. "I miss you that's all. You miss me, too." He wanted me to respond, but the MacDaniel woman's death distracted me, even from Gianni's flirtations.

He went on. "Take care of yourself. You know you can get hold of me anytime you need me."

He never gave up. A dense silence rose between us

After a minute he said, "Genevieve. You know how it is."

"I've got a problem right now, Gianni. It's the only thing on my mind."

His voice softened. "I love you." He raised his eyebrows, smiled, and stretched his arms out toward me.

"I love you, too. Thanks for all your help." I mouthed a kiss and touched End. I stared at the phone, then called Charlie.

"Giordano's not worried and he said you shouldn't either. It happens to every employer. He suggested setting up a fund for Becky's kids."

"God, Gen, that's the first positive thought I've heard all day. Thanks. I'll call the bank and open an account. I'll call Giordano and tell him thanks."

"Good idea, Charlie. I've gotta go now. My customers are already at their desks. If I get through to them now, I can get it over with before the news becomes gossip."

I made and fielded more than fifty calls that day. Customers, friends, Charlie every half hour, *The Clement Observer*, our local paper, Channel 13 out of Rochester, even freakin' WRUR public radio.

Jim Keough at the *Observer* had my cell number as a matter of course. I didn't want to, but I had to talk to him, my former boss. As he interviewed me, I cringed. I'd quit his paper one af-

ternoon before I started at American Tofu, when his hand circled around my back and landed on my breast while I worked
at the computer. I immediately deleted his entire weekly color
ad supplement and walked out.

The interview about the death was the first time I'd spo-
ken with him since. I'd enveloped myself with such anger and
distaste for him, that even in this one supermarket town, I'd
evaded him. Now, for the dead woman's sake, and for AT, I acted civil toward him. I told him I didn't know the woman, but I
was shocked and sad, and the company would do everything it
could for her family.

"I don't know any details. Call Charlie." Then my disgust at
him got the best of me.

"Don't call me back you creep if you know what's good for
you." I slammed the phone down. I'd never told anybody about
his roving hand, but the way I felt now, nothing would stop me
if he gave me or AT any bad press.

I called our customers. To a man and the two women, they
were sympathetic and expressed their concern. I told them
about the fund the company had set up to take care of the funeral expenses and to start an education account for the kids.

"That's the kind of thing I like about you, Genevieve," more
than one customer told me. "Always watching out for everyone.
Don't worry. We'll stick with you." I prayed they would, or we
were all finished with tofu.

***

I arrived home late that night, wiped out, to find Liam waiting
up, not happy that I'd canceled our dinner date.

"Mom, I walked into school today and everybody stared at
me like it was you who died."

"You told them I was fine?"

"Yeah. But I had to go to the principal's office. She asked me
if I wanted to take the day off. I said 'Sure' but she changed her
mind when I told her you wouldn't be home."

We talked about how sad everyone was. He knew one of the MacDaniel kids from his soccer league.

"Half the girls in school were crying all day," he said.

"Work is always dangerous, honey. Accidents happen all the time. All we can do now is try to help the family." Too late, I heard how Liam might think I was telling him I could have a bad accident just by being on the job.

He squirmed and his voice quavered. "Is it dangerous where you work? Ashley's dad got hurt at his place and has to sit in a wheelchair now."

I backpedaled to assure him I was always safe, but I wouldn't lie to him. He and I never misled each other.

"My job's the safest one in the company. I'm on the highway or in offices. When I'm in the car, I drive slow. When I'm in the office, I make sure I stay out of the way of people when they rush out the door at five o'clock."

He missed my poor excuse for humor and lay his head back on the couch. I sat next to him, pulled him against me, and lay my head back. We sat, our fingers interlaced, now and then squeezing reassurance to each other, giggling. How I love that boy.

****

At the funeral reception, Charlie played his usual Big Gorilla, strutting around like he was in charge of everybody's mourning, striding down the aisle between Becky's sisters, hugging them against his ribs as tight as he could, agony on his face. He and Nora and their children sat in the front row with Becky's family. Dozens of bouquets drenched the little church with a nauseating fragrance. Charlie had spent at least a thousand dollars on flowers.

I brought my camera to document the funeral for the family. Of all the sad gatherings I'd shot in my ten years of semi-professional photography, none were as gloomy as this.

We shut the factory down for the day and lowered the flag in honor of Becky. All our employees and their families showed up for the service, filling the pews with more worshipers than the church had seen for years.

The minister obviously didn't know Becky any better than I did. He mentioned her 'lively spirit' and 'enthusiasm for life' but he couldn't help moralizing with 'As you reap, so you sow," no doubt referring to her reputation as a party girl. Several heads nodded in agreement with the preacher.

After the service, the friends and family convened at the Grange for the reception. Charlie and Nora had spent another couple of thousand dollars on food and booze for the mourners, most of whom were morose tofu workers and their families. In American Tofu, the multicultural crew somehow formed bonds tighter than many families. Charlie's inclusive nature had something to do with it, the stability of the workforce helped.

Charlie sat at the head table trying to entice Becky's children to talk, but they kept their chins on their chests and barely moved.

After everyone had served themselves from the gourmet buffet I'd cajoled from Wegmans, our top supermarket customer, Charlie stood up. Dinner was a hit: the mourners had cleaned the platter of tofu-stuffed mushrooms with double Parmesan.

"This is the saddest time we can imagine. One of our own, a dear friend and a mother and a beautiful woman, not to mention a great worker and a dear friend."

He stammered and began to cry. I snatched a glimpse of Benko, one of the few in the room with dry eyes. He raised his brushy eyebrows and wiggled them at me and I smiled and looked away, feeling a confusing mix of sadness for Becky's kids and impatience with the whole scene.

You could almost taste pumpkin and cinnamon in the light and my body longed to leave with Benko and make the most of an afternoon off work. The police chief and his wife sat by themselves at a table near the door, watching everything, either keeping themselves at the border of the group so they could see everybody better, or paying their respects as official, but disinterested, town officials.

Charlie sipped something tan. Ginger ale? Whiskey? "The only thing that matters is that she comes back and we know we can't have that ..."

He drank again and I noticed many arms in the audience lifting glasses nearly in unison with Charlie.

"I'm not gonna speak a long time. All of you have a lot to say. Nora and I just want to announce a fund we're gonna start for Jolanda and Jonah. The Becky MacDaniel Children's Education Trust."

People nodded in appreciation. A few started clapping.

"No, no. Wait. We'll get the ball rolling with ten thousand dollars ... and ... Genevieve O'Connor. You all know her?" He pointed at me. "The greatest tofu saleswoman in history."

I wanted to scream at Charlie for his stupid badly-timed flattery, but when I smiled glumly and looked around with my lips turned down, real smiles came back at me from the women, along with flirty smirks from some of the men.

Half a dozen men winked at me. One of the warehouse guys raised his half-full glass, tipped it my way, and downed it, his eyes never leaving my face. I pinched my lips, raised my eyebrows, and shook my head, intending to express my sadness while showing him my appreciation for his salute, but keeping my distance.

Charlie continued. "Genevieve'll convince our customers to donate many more thousands for these beautiful little children here to go to college."

Charlie wavered again and pulled out his handkerchief. The two secretaries who sat beside me offered me tissue too so I could wipe my eyes.

A thunder of nose-blowing rolled through the room with a couple of extended booms. A large woman in her twenties wearing a scarlet and gold running suit blew a long set of tortured bass notes and rolled her head back and wailed.

Her friends leapt up from their seats and surrounded her, hugging her, shushing her but she resisted and howled louder.

Except for her weeping, the room fell silent. The woman moaned the words "Jo-nah" and "Jo-laaaan-da" over and over.

My eyes and everyone else's latched onto Becky's children. They both stared at the mourner with dry, hard eyes until Jolanda ran across the room, folding herself into the sobbing woman who wrapped her arms around the calm child and, shrieking one more time, buried her face in the little girl's neck.

I turned to check on Benko. He slouched in his chair, gazing straight ahead, his hands grasping his glass on the tabletop, ignoring the scene.

Becky's daughter ran back to her seat at the head table near Charlie and snuggled into her aunt's arms and the room came alive with a buzz of conversation.

"One more thing," Charlie said, almost shouting, "we're all pretty upset, but the most important thing for these kids, for our American Tofu family, we have to stick together, take care of each other. Remember. We're a family here."

A few voices called out "Yeah."

"Right, Charlie."

"Family."

Charlie raised both hands. "That's all from me. Now you all say beautiful things you have to say about our sad lost friend. Be good to each other."

Charlie sat down and put his head in his hands. The room went totally silent until someone started clapping again. Charlie's head bobbed up and he clapped back to the audience like a performer.

After a half-hour of speeches by Becky's friends, I said good-bye to the family. They held my arms and hands so tightly, thanking me as if I was going to make everything all right for them now that nothing would be right for a long time. The kids' faces held so much confusion and anger, I had to turn away before tears poured down my cheeks. I tried to smile at them and left the hall, avoiding any employees.

Nora followed me outside. We hugged and held each other for a moment.

"You holding up, Gen?"

"Yeah, all right. Did you see those kids? What will happen to them now?"

"Live with her sister, y'know, till they figure something out."

"You and Charlie are generous," I said, meaning it. They paid the best wages in the area and gave better benefits than any other business in town.

"We can't really afford it right now, but what can we do? Thank you for your help with the fund."

"It was Giordano's idea. I called him again and he gave another five thousand."

"How was that?" she asked, referring to my lingering feelings for Gianni.

"He still wants me. I miss him, but that's a past life. He accepts being my friend."

"Good. He's one of the company's best friends, too," she said. "Thanks to you." Tightening her lips, she went on, "Let me know if you need any help raising money for the kids' fund, all right?"

Nora, the boss's wife. Maybe the real boss, but I respected her. Charlie never faced any problems head-on. He would hint that something bothered him, or make some passive-aggressive remark, if he was upset with me. But Nora always spoke her mind, even if she was flaky as often as she was sharp.

"Thanks," I said. "Gotta go."

"By the way, thanks for taking pictures. I'm sure the family will be grateful."

"Maybe. They may not want these memories, but I'm sure our production staff will. They want to make a memorial."

We hugged good-bye and I drove home to meet Benko for an afternoon rendezvous, before Liam came home from school. We had two hours to play on a perfect afternoon.

# Chapter Five

## *Charlie*

# THE CHIEF AND
# THE EMPEROR

*I'm not worried now*
*I talked with everybody*
*no one knows a thing*

By the night following the medical exams ordered by Buhrman, all but one of our workers and managers had shown up and given fingerprints. Embarrassing scratches showed up on the backs and bottoms of three single women and one married man, but they obviously had nothing to do with Becky.

The scratch on my back had blurred but Buhrman insisted on sampling my DNA along with the others, but if I objected he'd point to my chin and elevate me to the top of his suspect list. The workers and I joked about our "love tattoos" and I think they held me in high regard for being not only a boss but for still having a lively sex life.

"Too bad but, my scratches have nothing to do with sex," I told the group of four as we sat around waiting for instructions.

"Sure, Mr. Greer," Stanley Pucánski said. "Nothing at all." The women tittered.

"I wish it did." I almost leered, getting into the spirit with them. "Well the one on my back, maybe. Twelve years of marriage, still having fun."

Everybody laughed, thrilled to hear such self-revelation from their boss. "The other one? My daughter punched her old man in the chin."

They stopped smiling.

"Wrestling with my kids." Everybody relaxed. "This whole thing's way too sad," I said.

"Wasn't nobody's fault," one of the women said. "The Chief's gone bonkers. It's the stupidest thing I ever heard of." Everyone agreed.

The newspaper came out the next morning with a chronicle of events since the death, steaming with lurid speculation about the flesh under Becky's fingernails and false sorrow about the fetus. The owners published an op-ed piece by one of the local ministers who decried the horrors of violence to the unborn, while ignoring the loss Becky's living children would have to endure.

Photos of our four scratched employees appeared under the caption "Ferocious Lovers Implicated in Death at American Tofu." The caption mentioned that the owner of the company was also examined for cuts and scrapes, but he declined to have his photo taken.

When I read that article and especially when I saw the pictures, I went berserk. I offered to help the workers sue the paper for infamy or libel or anything they wanted, it didn't matter how much it would cost.

None of them wanted to sue. They'd denied that the scratches had anything to do with lovemaking, but after talking it over, they decided they liked being known as "Ferocious Lovers." The photo and the caption appeared in several newspapers around the state.

One of the women searched every publication and web site in the country for signs of the picture. She posted a couple of dozen images from newspapers as far away as Vancouver, British Columbia on the internal company web site, printed them out, and pinned them to the employee bulletin board. Another Google search yielded the same photo in a Japanese business paper. The translated caption read "Tofu Transforms American Workers into Lovers with Appetites Like Man-eating Tigers."

Watching their *Ferocious Lovers* fame expand around the world distracted our employees for a little while from the serious business of Becky's death and the murder investigation. The DNA reports were delayed, but Buhrman cleared all but one of our workers of any connection with the death, though he said new information could change his mind.

As soon as Nora saw the photo and read the caption, she called me, furious that I hadn't told her about the exam and how my scratches had implicated me.

"You know what a DNA test for you means?"

"It's nothing. Protocol. I told you the Chief is riding his high horse. Nobody thinks it was a murder. You know as well as anybody."

"Wake up, Charlie. He's as good as accusing you."

"Of what? Nora, he's playing an intimidation game, is all. I go along with him, show no resistance, he calms down. I've got nothing to hide."

Her voice went flat. "Are you sure?"

"Of course I'm sure. What do you mean by that?"

"Where did you get the scratches?"

"Now you're accusing me?"

"I'm not accusing you. Just, like, where'd you get them?"

"Rissi bopped me on the chin while we were fooling around. Remember, I put them to bed so you could play cards at the club or whatever you do?"

She ignored my sarcasm. "What about the ones on your back?" "Oh, Jesus. Are you getting jealous?"

"I heard you told your workers I scratched you. Your hot little wifey."

"What am I supposed to tell them? I got kinky because my wife's never home?"

"We haven't touched each other for weeks, months. Why lie?"

"For God's sake. I was out in the country bushwacking. You know, I hike into the woods, pretend I'm lost, find my way back. You never want to go with me. Too many bugs."

"Oh. The woods. What happened?"

"I ran into one of those pines with broken low branches sticking out of the trunk. Lucky it jabbed the shoulder and not the eye."

*She knows something strange went down. Will she play along? She knows you're no hero. She thinks you're a clown.*

We didn't speak for a minute, both of us thinking over the story.

Finally, Nora said, "Whatever. You have to keep me informed about everything. Don't go off on some Charlie Greer crusade on this one. We have too much to lose."

"I'm taking it real easy. I'll let you know whatever happens. Don't worry."

"Way too much at stake, Charlie. The kids, the house. I'm in this with you. She was *our* employee, not just yours, y'know."

"Thanks, sweetie. You're the greatest. We'll let Buhrman play his game and the whole thing will blow over. When it's done, let's take a trip, maybe the Jazz festival in New Orleans like we always dream about. Your mom can stay with the kids—"

"We'll talk about it."

Neither of us spoke for a minute, not sure we wanted to go away with each other.

Nora broke the silence. "Call me before you make any big decisions about the Chief."

I hung up and sagged in my chair wondering whether I could really trust her to be with me, one hundred percent, no matter what happened now. She was my partner, more my business partner and my parenting partner, but no longer my romantic partner, but whatever happened would affect us equally. Except if anyone found out about Becky and me, I could lose everything unless I put it in Nora's name, and soon. Not yet.

For now, I had an employee who died and an ambitious cop trying to make something of a factory accident, and that's all anyone needed to know.

At least now Nora and I had the story about my scratches straight between us.

***

The one employee who didn't pass Buhrman's scrutiny was Chen, the Chinese tofu specialist. He became the main suspect by default—he disappeared two days after Becky died without letting his body be examined or giving fingerprints.

A huge sense of relief settled into the factory when Chen became Buhrman's suspect, even though most of the workers thought Becky had slipped because she was probably high. Buhrman continued his investigation by probing into everybody's private lives, even the semi-retired women who did nothing but the laundry two hours every night. Everybody started acting nervous. I'd walk through the factory and notice no smiles, everyone head-down, grim-mouthed, making tofu.

I called Benko into my office to learn what I could about Buhrman's interrogations.

"What's he asking our people? He may be stepping on our people's rights. Cops always think they can get away with that."

"Yeah. He don't ask much," Benko said. "Where we were. Did we know her. He asks all the men if they ever 'had relations' with her."

"Did anybody?" I'd heard rumors that she was a party girl, but I really doubted them. Becky liked to drink and dance, but she wasn't the type to sleep around.

"No. Nobody admitted it. The Chief's wants her boyfriend— he's prime suspect. More than Chen, I think. Lucky for her ex." "What do you mean?"

"Her last guy. Moved. Cleveland. Works nights at IBM. Good alibi."

"Anybody say anything that got the Chief's attention?" Even though he promised to keep me informed, Buhrman would never tell me the results of the interviews.

"Who knows? One thing, boss? Hate to say. He asked the women if Becky ever said anything about you. Positive. Negative. Anything."

I cleared my throat and sipped some Pelegrino. I kept a case of the water in my office while I tried to get off coffee. Didn't work but I liked the light bubbly feeling in my throat. I raised my eyebrows.

He said, "They all told him she liked you."

"Shit. I mean, of course she liked me. Everyone likes me."

"Take it easy, boss. That's right. They all like you, 'specially the women. Nice fizzy you drink."

"Did they tell Buhrman that?" I felt like a guilty politician for a minute, checking my poll ratings to see how far I could go before I lost ground with my people.

"Yeah."

I told Benko thanks and gave him a liter of Pelegrino to take back to his office. He'd told me a few things. Buhrman suspected me of some connection, but my employees—definitely the women would back me up.

Oddly, during Buhrman's inquiry, our factory productivity climbed like it never had. Waste material declined and our pounds produced per hour skyrocketed. I guess the workers tried harder than ever to be good for fear of becoming suspects or scapegoats of gossip.

My secretary buzzed my line and I answered the Chief's daily call.

"Greer, you've got to help turn the Chink up. He's gotta be the one. Why else would he disappear?"

"He might be," I said. "Chen worked here for a year and we never had any trouble from him, but it does seem strange." If Buhrman wanted a murder, Chen was the perfect suspect as far as I was concerned, especially since he'd be impossible to find. "Chinese workers come and go all the time. They circulate in and out of New York on something like an underground railroad."

"They have papers?"

"Sure, they're all legal. I mean they have some kind of shuttle. They work here, on farms, restaurants all over the state. Chen came on recommendation of a customer of mine. Maybe you should call some Chinese cops."

"I did already. They've put the word on the street in New York. Soon as he gets a paycheck, we'll grab him. I've got his social security tagged. By the way, we're checking your employee records. I hope everything's ship-shape."

The Chief's tough guy act wore on me but I had to put up with it. My lawyer told me to keep notes of everything Buhrman said or did in case any real trouble showed up.

Maybe I could catch him in a good old-fashioned procedural mistake.

*The Chief's no screw-up. He's a crime engineer, making sure every angle trues up.*

***

Making tofu is a hot, wet, messy business. Workers wear tall rubber boots, rubber aprons, rubber gloves, and ear plugs. Water flows constantly across the floor, steam pours out of kettles and coagulators sometimes rendering the production room into a tropical fog, while grinding and banging noises fill the air with a rolling thunder.

Despite the fact we paid wages twenty percent higher than other businesses in the whole of Upstate New York, we had trouble finding and keeping good production workers.

Chen had been the eighth or ninth tofu worker I'd hired on the recommendation of Chang Meng, the owner of Meng Produce, our second largest customer, and one of my mentors in business. All the workers were excellent, though they usually didn't stay in Clement for more than a few months.

Meng was one of the most powerful men in the New York produce market. At the office, we referred to him as "The Emperor of Hunts Point." He was more than a customer: He was an elder who planned to take me to Taiwan and who treated me like a relative; I knew his daughter very well; most importantly, he'd implied in his ambiguous way that he wanted to buy American Tofu, should I ever want to sell. I couldn't afford to jeopardize my relationship with Meng.

Each of the Chinese tofu-makers Meng sent me had been meticulous and hard-working and obedient. I liked them on the cleanup crew because they had a natural bent for sanitation. They never dirtied their uniforms. They seemed to float through the night-long soap and scalding water routine like albino ducks.

I gave Meng a call.

"Charlie, I don't know where he is. He could be in LA or Mexico City by now. I'll try to find out. Don't expect much. These guys have an underground railroad that I don't get involved in."

This was a real underground railroad, shifting illegals from city to city, state to state, no doubt for a percentage of their pay.

The next day, Meng called me with bad news about Chen. "We think he's in San Francisco already."

I felt the first relief I'd felt in weeks. We had a live suspect to engage the Chief.

"You'll never get him back," Meng said. "First, he's an illegal. He had all the right papers, but his name is not Chen. Nobody knows what it is. I'm sure he has a different name and new papers now."

"If you could find him, why can't the police?" I asked. "They'll have their contacts, too, won't they?"

"I found his trail, not him. If he wants to disappear," Meng pointed out, "it's the easiest thing in the world. See it from his point of view—he's an illegal. Doesn't speak English. Those farmers up where you live would love to hang a Chinaman. All the good jobs in the country are moving overseas—godless Chinks are easy to blame."

"Wait a minute, Meng," I said. "There's justice in the courts. He'd get a fair trial."

"Charlie, whether he killed the woman or not, you're on a wild goose chase. If you get too close, they just fly up into the sky and become stars." Meng's chuckle came through the phone like a cough. He was referring to my favorite Chinese fairy tale, the one my kids had memorized.

***

A few hours after I spoke with Meng, Buhrman showed up. If he didn't call, he'd taken to dropping by unannounced almost every day.

"Guess what?" he said, beaming a satisfied smile. "Chen's looking like our boy more and more. Did you check his papers real careful when you hired him?"

"We followed the legal procedure to the T," I said. "We're a professional company, Aaron. Maybe you think we make a strange product, but we have bank loans, a government contract. We pay as well as anybody in town. We do it right."

"Bet you do," he said, ignoring me. "Chen used false papers. Hsi Shin Chen of Long Island City, New York, is not the Chen you had in your factory. The deceased Mr. H. S. Chen ran a funeral home. Your boy stole his name and social security number." The Chief brayed out the information like a hound snapping at the heels of his prey.

*If Chen's illegal, Chief's caught you in a little crime. He's building his case on you, thinks it's just a matter of time.*

I played dumb. His information sounded solid, but the casual assertion that I knew Chen was an illegal let me know that Buhrman wanted to involve me. "How was I supposed to know his social security number is false?" I asked. "He showed us his card, we took his photo ID, he signed the papers. You can leave us out of this, Chief. Go find Chen if you think he did it."

"I'm doing everything I can. But why would he kill her? You have a reputation for getting to know your workers. What do you know about him?"

"I'm too busy to know everybody."

"Don't hide anything now. What about the dead woman. Mac-Daniel. You know her very well?"

He surprised me by the abrupt turn from talking about Chen. Where was he headed? I kept the conversation flowing, concealing my discomfort and playing along. "If they stay long enough, I talk to them at lunch or at our parties. She was a good worker. Talk to Gladonov if you want to know more."

"Every time I talk to him, I almost have to have a translator. These Russkies. Smart? Don't know right from wrong? Don't care either. Power hungry ex-commies. If I was you? I wouldn't trust him farther than you can throw a soybean." He laughed at his joke and clapped me on the shoulder.

"He's the best production manager I've had."

The Chief watched me through his laugh-wrinkles, expecting me to defend Benko's heritage so we could have an argument that I'd end up losing. I had to stop the Chief's immigrant-baiting. "As far as I can tell, he's honest and hard-working. Comes in all hours if we have a machine problem."

"Yeah. He might be the exception." The Chief blinked as if he had something in his eye, then shrugged. "I have to go down to Hunts Point tomorrow. Visit your Chink distributor. Maybe see Giordano, too." He sneered and stood up. "Good Italian company. Connected?"

If he thought he could force me to lose my temper and reveal something, I was not that dense. Giordano Brothers was our largest customer by far, a fifth-generation family-owned company. I had no idea if they were connected to the Mafia. I doubted it. Everything about them was far too elegant, especially Giordano himself. When did a Mafia don ever graduate from Princeton with an MBA from Harvard?

Maybe Buhrman thought old-fashioned orneriness went along with the hassle of a small-town murder investigation. Without replying to his insinuation about the ethics of my customers, I rose and came around from behind my desk to escort him out.

"You got yourself sleeping with some strange bedfellows, Greer," he said. "Makes you wonder how you keep the riffraff out of Clem when you can't even trust your employers. Not that I don't trust you, understand. I'm going over to immigration when I'm in the city. Maybe the FBI."

*The FBI? They can make a happy man cry.*

Panic surged in my chest. "Why get the FBI into this? I heard they're a bunch of clutzes when it comes to small town stuff. Fat Bureaucracy of Idiots."

Ignoring my sarcasm, he said, "Can't help it. Things're moving fast. Maybe some drug connection here. Chinese Mafia. Italian. Crossing state lines. Double murder. Everything. It's a big mess. Do you think I like spending my time this way?"

Buhrman grinned like a teenage boy who couldn't help bragging to his pals about last night's conquest in the back seat of his father's car.

I changed the subject. "By the way, Aaron. Whatever happened with the DNA analysis?"

He stared at me for a minute before he replied. "Had some problems with the equipment. Unreliable high tech stuff. DNA's fragile, y'know. Can't take heat, can't take too much pressure, but we'll get it. Moved it over to Cornell where they handle the big cases. I'll let you know, when we get something concrete. We'll find out whose baby it was."

"That'd be a good clue."

"That'd be the whole story, Greer." Burhman put his Chief's cap on and looked at the floor, thinking. My full-specturm fluorescent ceiling light glinted off the shiny ebony of the bill.

"Didn't you go to Loyola University?" he asked.

"Yeah. In Chicago."

"Know where the FBI gets most of its agents?"

"Where."

"Good Catholic schools in the Midwest. Notre Dame. Loyola. Hey, you might even get to see some of your own classmates when they come to town."

I laughed. "It's all about right and wrong."

***

As soon as Buhrman left, I called Meng, as a friend, to warn him. Even though Giordano Brothers was my biggest customer, I never felt as comfortable with Gianni Giordano as I did with Meng, especially since I never paid much attention to Giordano until Genevieve joined the company. She accepted my challenge and built his sales up from almost nothing to the cash cow that drives our profits.

With Meng's recent overtures about buying the company and our upcoming Taiwan trip, he'd become more than my business ally. He even sent his daughter, Shu Ling, to make an industrial film with American Tofu and me in the starring roles—we were nearly family.

Meng wanted our whole New York market, all of Giordano's business as well as the Asian part he handled and I didn't blame him, but I couldn't allow that unless he bought the whole company.

I treated him like a respected uncle without whose business my company would lose thirty percent of its sales and most of our profits. I had a dozen good reasons to warn him about Buhrman. Not only that, I had a moral obligation to call him.

"Ridiculous," Meng said. "I don't have time to waste with a petty investigation. You don't want him digging too deep here, anyway. Shu Ling wouldn't like it either."

Shu Ling? Did Meng know about me and his daughter? She'd promised he'd never find out about our slightly more than Platonic dalliance. We were always discreet, but he could know something. I had nothing to hide from him about her, except my lus,t and since when was unconsummated desire for a stunning woman unusual? Just because it was his daughter I was supposed to shut off my appreciation of female beauty?

I kept my mouth shut about Shu Ling. If I lied and denied a relationship with her, he'd lose respect for me, respect I'd worked hard to gain. If I admitted to anything other than business, Meng might have to forbid me to see her. American Tofu would be the loser.

We were in a fragile position. If I was him, right now with all the ruckus around the death, I would find another source of tofu, for a back-up supply. A simpler one, one he could control, or one he could use to control me.

Becky's death had given the Canadian company that had snapped at our heels for months a wide open door to our market. The only way I knew to keep the customers in our fold was to suck up to them ten times more than we already did. "Nurture the relationships," something Genevieve was a master of.

"I'll do what I can," I told Meng, pointedly not responding to his mention of Shu Ling.

Dealing with Buhrman had primed me for handling other interrogators. "Don't take Buhrman too seriously. American Tofu's personnel records are in perfect condition. T's crossed, i's dotted, every capital letter capitalized. The Chief has to huff and puff to show he's on the case. It'll blow over,"I said. "By the way. How is Shu Ling's film coming along?"

"You know better than I do, Charlie," he said, sounding exasperated. "Let's hope your Chief backs off soon. Chinese companies don't operate the same as Americans. He may have a little trouble understanding that."

"He's country, but he works hard." Why was I defending Buhrman to the most important man in American Tofu's, and by obvious extension, my life?

"I don't have to tell you Meng Produce doesn't enjoy annoyances like these."

With that phone call, my relationship with Meng became way too complicated. About two months before, his daughter and I cooled a strange non-affair that, the more I thought about it, the more I believed that Meng probably knew about. Worse, I had to assume, he may even have orchestrated it.

Meng had introduced Shu Ling to me, suggested that he'd help finance her film about the tofu business in the United

States, and he'd arranged for its distribution in the Orient if I allowed her to shoot some footage in my factory.

Selling me on the idea, he said, "Good for everybody's business, Charlie. More people know about you and tofu, the more sell." Reflecting on that, I realized he tried too hard to sell me on something obvious and that made me nervous.

Shu Ling flew into Clement last spring like the Chinese princess she was, and I fell for her as soon as she walked in my office door. She was about the same height as her father, about a foot shorter than me, but her gleaming black cowboy boots made her feel tall and graceful as a ballerina. She astonished me with her ebony eyes and her red suede jacket and deerskin pants.

Her round face loomed out of a thin, ebony halo of hair that seemed to lengthen her neck and lift her head slightly off her trim body. A long French braid pulled her hair back and emphasized her wide cheeks and broad chin. A tiny ruby nose stud told me that she was a totally modern American woman, independent from her family tradition.

The first thing I said after "Pleased to meet you" was something like "Hey, your nose stud matches the one in my ear." I heard myself speaking idiocy and knew I was lost.

She came to make a film for her class at NYU grad school and I thought I was supposed to be the star with star privileges but she wouldn't let me touch her. She flirted continuously, we went skinny dipping a couple times, she even stayed overnight at my house one night when Nora was home. But we never came closer than light hugs hello or good-bye, yet my entire body ached and hummed with desire for her.

My paranoid analysis of Meng's purpose in introducing Shu Ling to me: He wanted to own my business some day and get his hands on the millions of tofu dollars that flowed through my bank account every year. Meng knew I was married, not totally happy, but married. Still, he could possibly get me as a son-in-law, if certain things went his way. If I was him, and wanted to acquire a major piece of business, I'd have a few different strategies in place.

It all fit, too well. I expected our trip to Taiwan to reveal all, or at least the essence of his plan. Until then, I had to keep the Chief out of Meng's way.

***

Harold Fierst, my company attorney, had the reputation as the toughest business attorney in central upstate. He'd never lost a major case against the IRS or any state agency, and he had deep influence in Albany. His brother owned a New York City investment banking firm specializing in oddball but legitimate initial public offerings. If we stayed on our growth curve, they'd take our company public in five years and I'd never have to work again.

Harold had always taken care of not only our legal filings and contracts, but he made policy recommendations and oversaw our risk coverage. Next to me and Genevieve, he brought home American Tofu's biggest checks, worth every penny. The day after Becky died, he'd sent a man to interview all the employees about her and to take photographs of the accident site and the surroundings.

In his office a few days later, he advised, "Prudence, Charlie. We make a case of the MacDaniel woman as a careless worker, somebody who partied big the night before, a known drinker and pot smoker and who knows what heavy drugs. Didn't they bust a crystal meth lab out your way last year?"

"That was a down by the Finger Lakes, Harold. Long way from Clement."

"Close enough. Hell, we can almost prove she was so stoned out of her mind that she dived into that tank of beans just to enjoy the experience!"

He laughed but he didn't smile when he saw the disapproving scowl on my face. He cleared his throat.

"Sad business, but we gotta protect the company. I've seen ten million dollar settlements on less harmful industrial accidents. Somebody lost his big toe, for Christ's sake. Ten million bucks, the jury award."

I must have looked stunned because he followed with, "Don't worry. We appealed and got it down to four."

"Christ, Harold. Let's make sure all our i's are dotted, you know. Do what's right, what we have to."

"We got it covered, don't worry." He steepled his fingers, resting his chin on his thumbs.

"Do her kids get anything?" This was one of the main reasons I'd driven all the way to his office for a confidential, unrecorded talk.

"This is where you're brilliant, Mr. Greer," he said, sitting up straight in the cracked leather chair he'd inherited from his grandfather. "Remember those term life policies on your staff I suggested and you said, go for it?"

"Yeah? That was a good idea. We have terrific benefits."

"Her kids will get $50,000 each and the company gets $100,000 to cover legal and other expenses."

"Great news, Harold. I'd never have remembered that." The truth was, the memory of that policy had come to me like the breath of an angel. Due to the nature of the accident, the insurance company would pay out and everyone would see how much we cared for our employees. Any possible suspicion would slide away from me. The insurance payouts would also take care of Harold as he stymied any lawsuits Becky's relatives might feel tempted to file.

"We'll make sure the news gets out about what a caring and responsible employer AT is," he said.

*That's you, Chuck. So caring, especially when it's your body you're sharing.*

"That's true as you're the most expensive firm in Syracuse." I grinned at him. "Just for the heck of it, Harold, what will your fees be in this case?"

He steepled his fingers again, tensed them, and leaned forward. "I think you have enough. Unless we get into a protracted court case. I know you don't want that."

"Let's get this done."

"She was a drunk and a druggie and an incompetent mother. She partied when she had to go to work in two hours. No jury would award a penny to the family, especially since the company has always taken care of its own."

I cringed, acid crept up into my throat. He portrayed one of the sweetest women I'd ever known as some low-life bitch, and he'd never met her. She liked to party, but she always took care of her kids first. As far as I knew, anyway.

"One little collateral thing." He leaned back in his chair. "You'll have a premium increase but hey ... your umbrella policy covers you for most contingencies."

"Let's do what we have to do." I was in no mood to worry about a premium increase no matter how big. "By the way," I said, getting to the real purpose of my visit, "what did the District Attorney say about Buhrman's investigation?"

"Well, John's a friend, you know, and I can't ask for too many favors."

"I don't want any favors, Harold. Just fair treatment. We don't have a murder here. We have an industrial accident and a berserk cop who's trying to make a name for himself!" I stood up and started my patented pacing. "On my back!"

"Take it easy, Charlie. Sit down."

"I can't."

"John's not gonna give Buhrman any more resources. He thinks the case doesn't have enough merit."

"All right." The first good news I'd had.

"But he won't pull him off the investigation."

"Outrageous. Why not?"

Fierst sat back, smiling at me like I was a naive kid. "Buhrman's got a good reputation and John likes to give the nose to his up-and-comers. Remember that schoolteacher kiddie porn bust a few years back? John says if it wasn't for Buhrman, if he hadn't stuck with it when everyone else was ready to hang it up, they'd never have found the main guy behind it—that scumbag preacher in Troy."

"What's that have to do with anything? Buhrman's out there fucking with my business, calling in the FBI, harassing my customers. That's gotta stop."

"Take it easy, Charlie. Here's how it lays: If Buhrman makes a fool of himself, you're the good guy. The long-suffering employer who goes all out to do everything possible for the family of the deceased. Besides, Buhrman's doing all the work for us if it ever comes to trial." He leaned forward, his hands flat on his desk like a pastor issuing dogma. "Buhrman's got a future, and he knows it. He's not gonna go out on any limbs that could short-circuit his path up. Calm down, Charlie. You're taking this guy way too seriously."

Buhrman's finding the 'main guy behind it all' scared me more than anything. I knew he was stubborn and clever, in his fake-Columbo way, and he was building his reputation on obstinacy, the one thing I feared most. As long as Buhrman kept beating the bushes, you never know who would show up or what could trap me. That's how you get results in business or anywhere: keep knocking on doors.

Fierst broke into my thoughts "You pay me for advice, right?" I nodded.

"I don't give it unless I think you need it, you know that." I nodded again.

"You're a problem-solver, Charlie, but don't turn this into a problem. Be neutral, concerned, but don't get involved. See no evil, hear no evil, say no evil. Be a good guy and Buhrman will back off pretty soon."

I left Fierst's office more vulnerable to Buhrman than when I thought he was just a bumbling, ambitious cop building his ego and his exit strategy from Clement. My life, my marriage, my business had become as wobbly as cubes of tofu floating in a bowl of hot and sour soup.

# Chapter Six

## *Charlie*

# THE ART OF "MONKEY LOVE"

*even if it's the only way*
*you can love me,*
*whisper me a dream*

News of Becky's pregnancy drove my mind out of my body. I walked around in a constant state of hyperventilation. If my DNA matched the baby's, so long Charlie Greer. It wouldn't prove murder, or even manslaughter, but it would prove the end of everything. Even Clinton wouldn't have survived if Monica had died for any reason.

We'd only slept together a half a dozen times or so and the baby couldn't have been mine. I always used a condom, except maybe the first time, and I'm sure I did, too, even if I can't remember. I remember talking about AIDS, so I'm sure I used a rubber. Her old boyfriend must have knocked her up before they split.

Anyway, the timing was off for me to be the father, close, but Becky and I didn't start our affair until the end of June, after Shu Ling made it clear she'd never be my lover. When Becky came along, I found the perfect stand-in for Shu Ling and the necessary release valve for my horniness.

I really don't know how this whole thing could happen to me. When I puzzle it out, I want someone to blame: First, Nora, for shutting me out, then Meng, for setting me up with Shu Ling who heated me up to volcanic melt so when somebody like Becky showed up, somebody who shouldn't have started fooling around with her boss, I lost it.

The real cause of it all? Me, myself, I, the bumbling stud who let my craving for love—face it—for sex, turn me into an ape in a tree, my tail dangling, feeling for any branch to swing on or crotch to land on—if only Shu Ling had not been such a tease.

***

What started as a once-in-a-lifetime opportunity—having my company publicized all across American and Asia—ended up with me in love with the film-maker daughter of my favorite customer, in an obsessive lust that led me to make the stupidest decision of my life.

By the time Shu Ling finished shooting the footage she needed for her segment on American Tofu, testosterone ran my show. Any reasonable person, even me in my lucid moments, would tell me to grow up and keep my barn door closed, but sometimes, one thing builds on another and events take on a life of their own.

First, one humid spring night in Albany, Genevieve charged me up with about 400 amps of lust. The night she told me about her failed affair with Giordano was the night I almost wrecked my entire relationship with her. She probably would have left the company and taken half our customers with her if I'd insisted on getting what my little brain wanted.

That started when I challenged her to a tofu-selling contest. For five years, I'd been the greatest tofu salesman in America, I'm sure, because AT grew faster than any other tofu company, and not because we had the most capital behind us. I beat the bushes, cut deals, came up with half-brained marketing schemes that, with luck, worked. I spent thousands on tickets and dinners for my customers and their wives while I built AT's solid foundation of customers.

I tried not to show it, but I felt proud I'd created a company, but more. Before AT, people thought tofu was an esoteric inedible thing that came out of roach-ridden basement factories in Chinatown, probably made by serfs. My goal was to change all that, and change it I did.

Genevieve had early sales successes and I wanted her to become better than me—so I could take a break. I concocted a scheme: I told her if she sold more than me in a year, I'd send her on a trip anywhere she wanted to go. She agreed, on the condition that whoever lost had to do ten housekeeping chores for the other. Typical female humor, but my office always needed cleaning.

At the end of the year, she'd torched me, outsold me by fifty percent and the company made more money than I'd dreamed of. I suspected she did it by inviting Gianni Giordano into her bed in exchange for his becoming our biggest customer. She claimed they fell in love and the sales jump had nothing to do with their relationship, but I can't believe that. The guy's gonna return the favor, unless he's a cold bastard.

So, one night last spring, on an after-dinner stroll along the swollen river in Cleveland, she told me about their affair and their break-up. I half-expected the purpose of her revealing her affair was that she wanted me to replace him somehow.

Stupid as a teenager after two beers, I came on to her in the hotel room. She kissed me and let me graze her fully-clothed breast, but once I got serious, she shot me down. Later, she admitted that she encouraged me, 'allowed me,' she said, out of loneliness.

"I need comfort, Charlie," she said. "Not sex. Besides, what about Nora?"

"Nora and I don't sleep together any more," I said.

"You don't?"

"Twelve years of the same old person, I guess. Let's not go into it. I'm sorry about tonight."

"Forget it, Charlie."

I'm glad she stopped me. Nora's never yet questioned my relationship with Genevieve, so I counted on Genevieve to keep quiet. What would she have to gain by talking anyway? Still, from that watershed night on, my sexual longings sprouted like a field of dandelions just waiting for somebody like Shu Ling to meander by and pick them.

From the first day I met the Chinese woman, she teased me incessantly, calling me 'my Nobleman from the North Country,' insisting I treat the 'Peach Blossom Princess' like a 'tender bloom,' but she wouldn't let me close enough to show her how sensitive my fingers could be.

My infatuation with film stardom vanished to make room for my lust for her. On impulse, a few days into filming, while we sipped coffee after lunch, I said, "Shu Ling, I want to be your lover."

Her anthracite eyes bored into mine and she didn't smile. "My lover or just make love to me?"

That confused me. "Why not both?"

"I have a lover, Charlie. I don't need two."

I blurted out "I have a wife, I don't need two."

"You didn't ask me to marry you, did you?"

"You make me crazy. Nobody's ever twisted me up like this."

Shu Ling reached over and lay her cool fingers on the back of my hand, circling her nails in the hairs, sending shivers up my arm and over my shoulder into my skull and out the top of my scalp. I jumped an inch off my chair.

"Charlie, I like you a lot. We have chemistry, but wait a while. When the time comes, the film's done, we know each other a little better—I can teach you some special ways of being with a woman."

My boldness almost always worked. "What do you mean?"

"Ancient Chinese love teaching. *The Art of Monkey Love.* I'm no Adept, but I know enough."

I laughed. Things were moving my way. "Monkey love? I thought all monkeys did was play with themselves for the tourists at the zoo?"

She removed her fingers from my hand.

"I get it. This is the Year of the Monkey and it's something the Chinese do to celebrate?"

Shu Ling shook her head no, taking my question seriously.

My mind spun out, like it always does when I'm nervous, clowning around. "Do you have a different art for every year? After we do the 'Monkey,' can we go for the 'Dragon.' That's gotta be hot and heavenly."

"What are you talking about?"

"Just wondering if this art of love is why China has so many people?"

"I don't think so, Charlie. You know what? You're not ready."

Shu Ling stiffened her shoulders. "I shouldn't have brought it up." "What? I'm sorry. What did I do? I was just joking around." "You're näive, Charlie, but I'm not upset. You wait and maybe, if we still like each other—"

"We'll like each other."

Shu Ling slid her chair back and came around the table, holding her tiny hand out, summoning me up. Taking it in both of mine, I drew myself close to her, inhaling her compelling fragrance, a heady mix of gardenia and spicy incense.

"Patience, Charlie. Waiting is the number one Taoist virtue." She laughed and let my hand drop and turned toward the exit. "Let's go back to work."

I believed she'd follow through with her promise so I had no choice but to enjoy the delay. I'd call it subtle lingering foreplay.

"No problem, Shu Ling. I get it. The first step in Monkey Love is called 'Filling the Reservoir.'"

She laughed and slapped my arm. "Not really, but if that works for you."

"It's rising fast. I'll let you know when we have to open the sluice."

The regular and only lightning rod for my sexual charge for all these years of marriage was Nora, and I'd done a damn good job of repressing my natural longings for other women. But lately her moods had become so changeable and our lovemaking, as mind-blowing as it sometimes was, happened so erratically I couldn't depend on her at all that summer. Now, my infatuation with Shu Ling prevented me from courting Nora the way I should have, if I really wanted her as badly as I claimed in our couples therapy.

Shu Ling and I talked on the phone daily the two weeks after her first visit. We talked so often that I began to feel closer to her in some ways than I was to Nora. But she let my lust rage unrequited, until too late, she gave me some hope of respite. By then, my patience worn thin, my reservoir overflowing and threatening to flood the whole valley, I started monkeying around with Becky.

***

My folly with Becky started the night after our annual American Tofu summer solstice party. I'd name the party after whatever Chinese Year we were in. This year, I invited the AT employees to come out to the park for an afternoon to "Monkey Around with Tofu."

We passed an afternoon at the local state park swimming, playing softball and Frisbee, eating endless forms of tofu salads and hot dogs, cakes and cookies. I'd ordered special desserts from our local ice cream shop: tofu ice cream banana splits drizzled with hot fudge and salted peanuts. We called them "Monkey Tails." The crew polished off the keg of beer and, at sunset, they migrated to the office manager's house for dancing and more drinking.

Nora went home with the kids, but I felt it was my duty as owner to continue sharing the fun with my employees. I'd paced my drinking so, at midnight, when the party dissolved, I volunteered to be a designated driver. Four inebriated workers, led by Becky MacDaniel, staggered to my car. I dropped the other three off first.

Becky had partly sobered up by the time we arrived at her yard. She invited me in for a nightcap and I accepted, sober and feeling the good feeling you get as leader of a clan that knows how to party together.

She offered me some hashish she'd just received from her cousin in Montreal. I didn't want to appear stodgy, so, following my policy of appreciating one's employees and in the entrepreneurial spirit of venturing into unexplored territories where you never knew what opportunities you'd find, I accepted.

She was a cute redhead, a little wide in the hips, but hardworking and cheerful. Sweet. She was one of the women I'd noticed and cultivated a collegial relationship with, in hopes that she'd seek a promotion inside the company. Keeping employees was much cheaper and better for the long-term morale than always hiring new people.

Still, I hesitated. "You can't get addicted to this, can you?"

"C'mon, Charlie, it's hash. Everybody knows it's medicine. Good for you. I wouldn't touch ice or crack. Nothing hard." She glanced at my lap when she said this and Mr. Jones got the signal to stand up and wave, but I crossed my legs. Still, her husky voice lured me, as if she knew about things I didn't, things I needed to learn.

*She'll teach you how to play. But how much d'you wanna pay?*

"I've never even smoked cigarettes," I said.

"Hash's smoother than cigarettes, if you take it easy." She inhaled from a polished wooden tube with a dull black bowl on the end. "Your turn."

*'Your turn.' You wanna burn?*

I accepted the pipe and sipped sweet smoke, letting it roll over my tongue and down my throat.

Becky coughed a cloud of smoke into my face and doubled over, laughing. "Don't be a sniffer like a puppy, Charlie. Drag it in deep and hold it down like a big dog." She hooted.

I sucked and held smoke in for what seemed like half an hour. I'd never smoked hashish before. Like everyone, I'd had plenty of chances, but booze got me high enough, and I knew how to control my alcohol buzz.

Becky put some drum music on her CD player, sat me down on the floor of the living room, and we passed the pipe back and forth. After three puffs, her face became radiant, more beautiful than Shu Ling and Nora put together.

Her skin looked silky and creamy, tinted with peach and strawberry. Her eyes twinkled and invited me to come closer. The entire universe shrunk down to the sapphire color of those eyes. I lost myself staring into them for an hour or an eternity. Never before in my life had I had the experience of seeing into someone's soul.

She touched my cheek with her fingers and the next thing I knew, we were rolling naked on the floor, laughing and hollering, pounding our fists into the carpet in time to the drumming on the CD. For a moment, I wondered where my clothes went and I scanned the room for them. My aloha shirt and cut-offs lay piled in a mound with her crimson blouse and leopard panties, shimmering tropical blossoms all tangled up and lit with animal light.

Becky tugged me into her room and we tumbled onto the bed. I had no protection with me. The hashish had burned off all my inhibitions but I knew enough to check with her.

"Do you have condoms?" I asked.

"Sure thing."

I said, "Don't worry. My annual physical included an HIV test and I was negative, I mean, I passed."

She laughed and said, "Me, too. So far, so good."

The "so far" scared me a little but I got it and we belly-laughed and pounded the bed. Afterward, I told Becky that the sex with her had been my best ever. The next morning, however, all I remembered was the oniony smell of her breath in my mouth as I listened to myself sneaking up the squeaky back stairs to my house while an owl hooted in the woods out back. I didn't remember disposing of a condom.

I came back to her several times during the summer, for laughs, wine, hashish, and sex. She must have learned by August that she was pregnant, but she never offered to skip the rubber. I wouldn't have, anyway.

***

During my affair with Becky, and after, no one in the company's warehouse or factory ever regarded me with anything other than respect, so I presumed that she'd kept our secret. I'd bought her a few candles and some things for her kitchen, but nothing personal or with my name on it.

Her kids were never home when I visited and they didn't recognize me at the funeral. I worried a little about my fingerprints, but we spent so little time at her place. If Buhrman dusted everywhere in her house for fingerprints, I might have a problem, but I hoped that Becky's birthday bash the night before she died would have smeared over any evidence of my presence.

***

At first, I thought the only reason I'd made love to Becky was for sexual release. When we got closer, I realized I needed a companion, someone to talk to, to let down my guard with. Becky and I had an honest relationship, no pretenses, no demands, and we had so much fun. Not like the other two women in my intimate life.

Shu Ling's flirting had tortured me and Nora was barely available. Her new passion for golf kept her at the country club most afternoons and late into many nights, drinking and playing cards with her golfing pals.

But as long as Nora was happy, I had my freedom. She received her share of the abundant funds American Tofu earned and she had total control of our family checkbook. I didn't need it because the business paid almost all of my expenses and gave me plenty of "walk-around" money. The talks Nora and I had in therapy compensated for that summer's absence of regular conversation and physical contact. We both seemed happy.

***

One sweltering night that July, a few weeks after I had taken up with Becky, I had to stay in New York the night before an early meeting. Shu Ling invited me over to view updates of film segments she'd shot on a recent trip to California, the real center of the tofu industry.

"You're calm, Charlie. I like you when you're not so hyped up," she said. "Did you start meditating?"

"Sort of." Sleeping with Becky helped keep me poised around other women, especially Shu Ling. I was tempted for a minute to tell her about Becky to add spritz to the evening. If I let her know that I was taking care of my sexual self quite well, thank you, perhaps she'd desire me more.

*Don't trust her. All you can count on is your lust for her.*

True, so far. But I'm an optimist, if I'm anything.

I kept my mouth shut about my new lover. That proved to be one of my wisest decisions ever. "I told myself I'm going to love you no matter whether we go to bed or not," I said. "I don't need to prove anything. I don't need anything from you. I enjoy being with you. Mature, isn't it?"

"I guess," she said. "Sounds boring. Did you give up on me?" She scooted close to me and, putting her arm around my neck, she kissed me on the ear.

I turned to kiss her, but she pulled back.

"No. I like it fraternal. It's got fizz that way. I have a boyfriend, Charlie. He wouldn't like it if we did anything."

I stood up. "Why are you teasing me then?"

"Let's just play," she said, ignoring my irritation. "Same ground rules as when we go swimming—naked but no fondling. Touching's allowed. No intercourse. You don't need penetration to really express and receive love."

"You ever hear of the Chinese Water torture? This is worse."

"Shut up. It's all part of Monkey Love. You should pay better attention—I've been teaching you all along. It's all about communication, connection."

"I wish I'd known."

"You knew. You got the essence, the non-verbal part."

"I get it. That's the Monkey part. The non-verbal," I said, puffing out my upper lip and mimicking monkey squeals.

"Could be."

I tried to tickle her but she shifted away. Scooting after her, I said, "I googled Monkey Love and I came up with some web sites I didn't want traces of on my computer."

"It's not about sex with animals. Give me a break."

"It's about the fact that chimpanzees and humans have 99.4% the same DNA. We're kissing cousins. The bonobos, too. You know, the monkeys who make love, not war? Every bonobo does it with all the others. They're not the shy types like me when it comes to sex."

"You're a gas, Charlie."

"Just the facts, ma'am. Just the facts."

Shu Ling wrinkled her nose as if she couldn't believe me. "Good research. You're a natural student."

I grinned, half-embarrassed, half-enthusiastic. I didn't know whether she was putting me down or teasing until she stood up and held out her hand.

"You want to stay here and jabber or do you want to come into my room and learn about real communication?"

I'd been waiting for that invitation ever since she soared into my office in the spring. I followed her hand-in-hand like her toy, a willing, salivating pet. I was out of control and I didn't care.

We sat down side by side on her black silk-quilted bed, our thighs brushing. I reached out to unbutton her blouse and she flicked my hand away.

"Wait." She turned to me and said, her voice dry and serious, "I'm going to teach you to make love without touching genitals, with clothes on."

I slumped and pouted, intentionally melodramatic. Hoping to inject light-heartedness into what was becoming schoolish, I said "We call that foreplay."

"Do you call it foreplay when you explode in ecstasy?"

"Do you mean, come?"

"Mmmm, yes ... " she hesitated. "Sometimes that's part of it. I think of orgasm as more of a distraction."

"I don't get it, but let's go."

"Patience. Tonight I'm going to teach you 'Marmoset Ears.' If that works out, the next time you can learn about 'Orangutan Toes.' If you're still a good boy ... I'll show you 'Bonobo Bellies.'"

"Bonobos? I knew I was onto something. Research pays." I tried to tickle her again but she wiggled away. "Let's start with them. I already know something about bellies."

She put her finger to my lips, shushing me. "Those aren't the Chinese names, Charlie. I made them up just now."

"They work for me."

"Relax. Nothing urgent here. Anyway, you're a virgin."

"I wish—"

"I don't want to hurt you."

We never did see her film clips because for the next hour, Shu Ling elevated the game of monkey play to a fine aural erotic art: pinches, nips, groans, flickering licks and countless other touches with her teeth and tongue stimulated my lobes and whorls and inner recesses in a way that hyper-sensitized my entire body.

"Your ears are like a woman's secret parts," she whispered. "Silky, moist, tremulous."

She strummed toneless string instruments that sounded like telephone wires buzzing and murmured love poems in Chinese. She demonstrated acupressure-point nibbling and writhed and moaned when I practiced my new learning on her.

I didn't arrive at any explosion, but when I left for my hotel at midnight, city night sounds sang in a symphony of horns tooting, tires fluting, voices harmonizing a cappella. My body hummed a summer melody that was part steam, part melted butterscotch. I gasped awake in the middle of the night, a chorus of birds and blowing leaves tingling in my ears, my pelvis shuddering. I called Shu Ling immediately, gasping my thanks into her voice mail.

When I checked my own voice mail the next morning, she'd left me a puzzling message, some Taoist teaching, no doubt.

"Sorry you lost it," she said in her breathy accent. "I didn't mean to go overboard. Next time I'll remember you're still a fledgling. Ciao, little gander."

We didn't find the time or place in August to have the next session on 'Orangutan Toes and Simian Soles.' She was traveling and frankly, I'd lost interest: Becky had become primal woman enough for me.

***

Three months after Shu Ling and I played Marmoset and five weeks after Becky died, I felt mugged by the Chief's investigation. It often felt more like a persecution: browbeating calls to me, demands on my staff, intimations in the local paper about a "highly placed" suspect.

One morning, I aimed my car south and slogged down the Interstate toward an advertising meeting in New York and dinner with Shu Ling. I braved the lashings of the tail of an autumn Caribbean hurricane that kept all but the most desperate drivers off the road.

The highway flooded with streams and puddles, rocking my Cherokee like a small outboard on a windy lake. Confused thoughts splattered across my mind while muddy water splashed over my windshield and rain blurred headlights into haloes too dim to illuminate the lane markers.

By the time I arrived at Shu Ling's apartment on Mott Street, the rain had stopped and the city basked in a balmy fall blessing. The New York air sparkled and the traffic whistled by like it was carrying people eager to get to a spontaneous city-wide party.

I looked forward to an afternoon of relaxation with the Princess. I needed to blank out my fears and worries, even the facts, from my mind. I'd told Shu Ling about the death right after it happened, and during the weeks since the investigation began, we talked a half-dozen times. She was always caring and her words never failed to strengthen my resolve.

I rang her bell and sped up the stairs the second she buzzed me in. Pushing open her unlocked door, I found her in the kitchen and we hugged each other chest-to-chest and thigh-to-thigh. I grinned at her, even as she pushed me gently away, pointing me to the living room.

She'd ordered in ravioli and salad for lunch and we opened a bottle of Chianti, a prelude, I thought, to one of her arcane love lessons where  all was pleasure and bliss. We sat down on her couch to an indoor picnic.

"I think it's going to be all right," I said between mouthfuls of mesclun spiced with lots of raddichio. We sat close to each other, our plates on the glass coffee table. "Your father and our other customers aren't too worried."

"I'm worried, though. I'm worried for you," she said, putting her plate down and scanning my face, as if checking for signs of deterioration.

"I'll survive."

"You'll survive. But what about your family and everyone else? Did you know your police chief called my father a bunch of times? He says the death was no accident."

"When did Buhrman call again?" My body went cold at the news. One of my knees started shaking. "Why didn't you tell me?"

"I don't know. Yesterday? My father mentioned it last night. He called just to say hello and talk about the film. He said 'Things look sticky for Charlie.'"

"Buhrman pisses me off. He's making everybody nervous."
"What will you do if it is a murder?"

Shu Ling's interest tempted me to tell her then and there about my affair with Becky.

*If Meng finds out, bye bye American Tofu pie. He'll wreck your business and suck you dry.*

Jiminy's words rang true, as usual. This time I listened. I swallowed and changed the focus of our talk.

"I don't know," I said, not looking directly at Shu Ling. "Do you think your father had anything to do with this?"

"Charlie! Are you crazy? He's rough, but he'd never get involved. What's the matter with you?"

"I don't know. I'm really confused." Telling her that little obvious truth made me feel better.

"I guess you are. You'd better talk to my father. He's probably your best ally. Maybe he can help."

"How?"

"He's got contacts everywhere."

"I'll talk to him about it on our trip. It's only two weeks before we leave."

Either she had no clue that her father would do anything to achieve his business goals or her acting could win her awards. Of all the businessmen I knew, I'd identified Meng as the one whose style I could mimic to help get me through the Buhrman crisis: Play it close to the vest, stay above the fray.

"Can we preview your film?"

She inserted the DVD and, relieved to stop thinking about Meng, I watched.

Shu Ling had done everything to make her straightforward industrial film as upbeat and entertaining as possible, but as we watched the final segments showing California and Canadian tofu factories, I started feeling depressed.

I should have waited until the cloud of the investigation cleared, because I was in no mood to face the realities of my company's true inferiority in the harsh world of the tofu wars.

The huge factories all had modern high-tech equipment and energetic, Asian, robotic, sanitized workers. I suspected that they could make tofu a lot cheaper, and probably with better quality, than we could, ship it east, and take most of American Tofu's business if we showed the slightest vulnerability in our position or reputation.

I desperately needed a bottle of hot sake and a lesson in "Orangutan Toes," but Shu Ling said I was too upset. Besides, she had a dinner date.

I dragged myself to my hotel, ordered room service, and ate a tasteless meal. I lay unable to sleep, wondering if Shu Ling would forgive me for accusing her father.

By late evening, the hurricane circled back around Manhattan, pouring dense sheets of water onto the night city. They snaked across my hotel room window like thick vines probing the sash, seeking a way inside.

# Chapter Seven

## *Charlie*

# HOTEL DELIGHT

*in scarlet Taipei*
*slave girl barbers rub*
*bald heads—all shapes, all sizes*

Meng and I left from JFK for Taipei two weeks later on a Taiwan Airlines 747. This would be my first chance to immerse myself in Chinese culture. Ever since I read Sun Tzu's *The Art of War* and applied its lessons to running my business with incredible success, ancient China has obsessed my thinking.

Its ancient discovery, tofu, supports my family and dozens of others, bringing health to hearts and hot-flash free menopause to women. Its drugless medicine—acupuncture, herbs, qi gong thousands of years of healing without government boards approving treatments, and without doctors becoming rich on the pain of their patients. Ancient Chinese wisdom can't be compared with our modern thinking. They practiced *wu wei*, non-action. As I understand it, you wait until the thing you want happens by itself. You have to get your mind in the right place, but once it's there, you're in the flow, and the flow is the way the universe operates. I've heard it said you have to surf the flow.

*Wu wei* worked in my negotiations. If somebody objected to something I proposed, I'd wait. If the flow washed their acceptance my way, I soaked it up and we moved on. If not, I'd leave the table, until they called me back with an offer.

But since Becky died, my flow had run underground and I had just enough energy to focus all my *wu wei* on avoiding the Chief's suspicions.

Relaxing in comfortable first class seats as the plane rose over the North Atlantic, heading over the top of the world, Meng and I sat side by side. I wanted to impress Meng with the scope of my business ambition, so I revealed my hopes and dreams.

"Henry Ford was one of the greatest businessmen America ever produced," I said. "He created the assembly line. He was clever. Did you know he demanded that parts be shipped to him in a certain kind of box? When the box arrived, he dismantled it and bolted it to the car for running boards?"

"He sounds Chinese," Meng said, chuckling, setting down his Taipei newspaper and raising his leather recliner from nap position.

"He made one kind of car in one color for years. It was cheap, simple, everyone could have one. That's how he single-handedly created the auto industry. The whole economy of the world can thank him."

"True. Everyone wants a car."

"Yeah. Think about the oil and gas companies. What about the steel and rubber and glass and computer companies. The people who build and maintain roads. Advertising agencies. TV. Government. Everything."

"He did appear at a point of high industrial leverage in America," Meng said, sounding like a professor.

"Well, the point is not about his cars. It's about soybeans. He made a car entirely out of soybeans. Soybean oil, I mean, turned into plastic."

Meng listened carefully, focusing on my eyes.

"In 1934, at the World's Fair in Chicago, he served a 13-course dinner. Everything was made from soy. Appetizers, milk, meat, dessert. Everybody raved."

"Genius doesn't confine itself to one field, does it?" Meng said. "Some of my heroes were rulers, poets, swordsmen, inventors. Flowers of human evolution. I myself only dabble in painting and piano."

"I don't do much else besides business," I admitted. "A little poetry. My dream is to carry on Henry Ford's vision. Right now, I make one color, one flavor, two sizes of tofu. It's cheap. Everyone can use it. It's democracy's ideal food. The Model A of the dining room table."

"Good luck. Maybe your research in Taiwan will help you become the Henry Ford of tofu. Excuse me," he smiled, "I should say the Charlie Greer of tofu. You'll bring soy to the whole world, just like Ford brought cars."

A flash zinged through my mind—the flash I'd been waiting for. *Soy to the whole world.* Right there on the 747, the future of American Tofu popped into my head. *Wu wei* in action. Oops, I mean, non-action.

We'd combine modern American farming and food processing technology with ancient Chinese healing cuisine and military strategy. Using the most creative, flamboyant marketing talent in New York, American Tofu would make its way onto every table in the U.S., and beyond.

We'd call our marketing campaign "Soy to the World." I'd copyright the words and create TV ads no one could forget. The trip had already paid for itself.

*Soy to the world? Not your idea. It came from the dead girl.*

He's right. I'd buried the idea with Becky. It started with her asking me a question.

She had a day off, the kids were at school until 3. I took a long lunch at her house. We made love and lay there in bliss. Becky turned over on her back beside me and said, "What's your biggest dream? What would you do if you weren't afraid to fail?"

She was always reading self-help books and practicing their techniques on me. Usually I'd tease her about trying to change me or hypnotize me to have me under her control.

She'd laugh. "Don't worry. I'd never do that. Besides, I already have you under my control." I'd scrunch up my face like I was mad and tickle her until she'd squirm and kick and break free.

This time, I took her seriously. I thought about two seconds and blurted, "People all over the planet would eat tofu. Maybe not American Tofu. Maybe Kenyan or Brazilian. I'd set up factories everywhere, hire millions of people. It would change everything."

"That's pretty big. Tofu everywhere. Wow. I would never think up such a thing."

"You know, if you thought about tofu twenty four seven the way I do, you'd probably want to see everybody in the world eating tofu. We'd make lots of other soy foods and drinks. Soy all over would solve war, climate change, no more haves and have-nots."

Becky lay silent for a moment, then said, "Soy all over the world. Hmmm." She turned her head to me, her lush brown eyes twinkling. "Soy to the world."

"That's it," I said, taking her seriously. "Soy to the world." "Sounds like the Christmas song. 'Joy to the world.'"

Her rhyming got me going. "Hey. Cool. Want to write the song? 'Soy to the world.' We could make it American Tofu's anthem." "You're ambitious, Mr. Greer," she said.

Becky was a teaser, too. She called me "Mr. Greer" whenever she wanted to mock my upperclass standing. She called us "Mr. Greer and Little Becky."

When Becky called me "Mr. Greer," she was inviting me to play the game where she became the boss and I worked for her, doing whatever she commanded—from doing her dishes to trying something taboo in bed. This time, the idea of international tofu factories held my full attention.

"I guess I'm ambitious," I said. "I don't think of it that way. It's a mission. It's purpose. Something bigger than me."

Becky sat up and crossed her legs. She looked me in the eyes. "So you have been listening to me—you have a purpose, just like the CD said."

When I remember her sitting that way, naked, her lips pursed, her hair disheveled, her eyes focused on mine like she was trying to understand, nodding her head, my throat thickens. I feel tears rising behind my eyes. She was the most perfect gift of a woman I'd ever met. I missed her in my whole soul, like I'd never missed anybody.

I had to stand up and make my way to the plane's water closet where I sat on the lid of the toilet seat and let the tears pour out. I cried and groaned for a minute or two, then splashed water on my face. Once my eyes cleared up, I strode back to my seat.

At that minute, 37,000 feet in the air, somewhere over the Pacific, I decided the most important thing I could do with my life was to make "Soy to the world" come true. It would change the world, make a lot of money, assure my kids and her kids a happy future. And Becky would be at the heart of it.

Before she died, I wrote the song "Soy to the world" and sang it to her, off key but it sounded nice, she said. We sang a couple of duets and were starting to get good.

At Becky's memorial service, I handed out copies of the song to everyone, telling them Becky had composed it and given it me a week before she died. Everyone thought it was a perfect memorial all of us could share.

"It's beautiful." somebody said. "So sad."

***

Like all my dealings with Meng, the Taiwan trip became a mixed blessing. When we landed, I lifted my hundred pound case of samples onto a pushcart. A sharp pain stabbed me in my kidneys and I went to my knees. I staggered upright, but my lower back hurt so badly that I could barely walk.

Once I limped through customs, a perfunctory stamping of both our passports, Meng deposited me at the "Hotel Delight" in downtown Taipei. We made a date for dinner the next night, but he called an hour later and postponed dinner for a week. "I'm sorry, Charlie. I have to go down south and meet with some new suppliers. They're having problems with a project we're counting on."

"I'm sorry, too, Meng. I don't know what I'll do."

"I told William Woo Ai to be on call for you, if you need anything. Reach him through my Taipei office. You're enterprising, I'm not worried about you."

"Good luck with your suppliers, Meng. See you in a week."

"I'll call in a few days. Till then, enjoy yourself. Make sure you try The Golden Dragon restaurant. They have the most delicious dim sum I've ever eaten."

"Looking forward to that," I said. "Next week then?"

"Good, Charlie. Enjoy yourself. You might be surprised what a good time you can have in Taipei."

Meng had given me a guidebook and a list written in Chinese of restaurants, museums, and temples. He told me to show any cab driver the list if I needed help. Maybe I could buy a Chinese/English phrase book and surprise Meng with my language facility when we got together for dinner.

A sour taste of panic at being alone for so long rose into my mouth, but I washed it back with a Dong Qi beer from the refrigerator. I didn't really want a week of solitude, but I decided I ought to take advantage of it to get a perspective on things, maybe come up with some inspiration about how to move the Chief to give up the case.

When I rolled out of bed the next morning, my body immediately jackknifed, falling hard onto the floor. My head slammed into my knees, my stomach retching as a violent spasm jolted my lower back. I worked an hour to relax the muscles and to crawl back into bed.

I'd told Meng I wanted to stay in a hotel that natives used. Since I couldn't speak or read Chinese when I groaned into the desk service phone, none of the hotel staff understood what I wanted. I dialed Meng's Taipei office but hung up before his secretary answered. No need to play a weakling.

The back pain, the muggy Taiwanese weather, my exhaustion from the trip, and the spasms every time I moved sapped my will. I lay in bed staring at the lone American TV channel and swallowing whatever food the staff left at my door.

I didn't feel like calling the factory and complaining. They needed to think I was out conquering the Orient for American Tofu. Nora had taken the kids hiking in the mountains while I was gone, so I couldn't call her.

I could have called Nora's cell phone, I guess. I didn't want her to know I was hurting as bad as I was. At that point in our marriage, I was pretty sure she didn't have much comfort in her heart for me anyway. I wondered if she had sniffed out something about my relationship with Becky. I'd never let on I'd had anything to do with Becky, but Nora seemed angry with me all the time. She was the one person I should be able to count on, but she kept her distance.

I lay on my back there in the Delight Hotel, listening to tropical showers drizzle off and on, half-paralyzed, alone as a beached whale. I had nothing to do except worry that somebody would come forward to the Chief with the news that they saw me with Becky the night she died. Or they'd seen us together sometime, anytime. It didn't make a difference which because I'd denied knowing her as anyone other than an employee. Still, in a small town, you bump into people you know in the grocery store or at the gas station all the time. So what if someone saw us together once or twice?

***

Nora called the second day of my incarceration in the hotel room. I groaned when I turned over to pick up the phone.

"How's it going, Charlie?"

For some reason I didn't want to tell her I was hurt. I wondered if I waited on purpose to throw my back out until I was half a world away from Nora. If I did it at home, she'd either ignore me or make such a big deal of taking care of me, I'd feel guilty for feeling bad.

"Not much happening so far. Meng's been busy so I just hang out, waiting."

"How's Taipei?"

"Noisy. What's going on with the Chief? Did he close the case yet?"

"Naw. He's called everybody in for a second round of interviews. I can't believe it, y'know. I'm scheduled for tomorrow."

"Jesus. Think he's up to something now I'm out of town?"

"Why would he? Guess what? I think he's, like, a dry drunk on a binge. An investigation binge."

I laughed. "Good insight. I hope you're right."

"Seriously. Deborah thinks so."

"The hundred fifty dollar an hour therapist? I guess she knows what she's talking about," I said, not eager to get into therapy-talk.

"She thinks we're under too much stress, y'know."

"Nothing that getting the Chief off my back won't solve. Howie the kids? I miss them."

"Rissi got a part in her kindergarten play, 'Three Billy Goats Gruff.' She's our little starlet, running around the house screaming and fainting, expecting me to clap every time she falls down."

"What do you mean?"

Nora laughed. "She's the little baby goat the trolls scare. All she has to do is scream and swoon."

"I can't wait to see the play. Tell her I'll be there. What's Chuckie up to?"

"Should I tell you? He's so proud he wanted to be the one to tell you he won the second grade spelling prize."

Thank God. Kids' lives go on no matter what hurricanes blow through the parent world. "You tell me and he can tell me, too, when I call on Saturday."

"Well, he was the only kid in his class who could spell 'friend.' Everyone else transposed the i and the e."

"Wow. Good thing he's your son, Nora. I'm not sure I could spell it right today."

"You could, Charlie. Are you taking care of yourself?"

"Best I can. I always do, you know."

"I mean, the stress and all. You've been a wreck."

Nora was right but, despite the pain, I was feeling a lot calmer than before I left Clement. "It's a good break here. I'll tell you all about it when I get back. How are you doing?" I asked, feeling real concern and wanting her to hear it.

"I'm fine. Too rainy for much golf these days, but I'm working with Genevieve on some projects." Nora sounded tired.

"Good. How's she? How're sales holding up?"

"Business is fine," she said. "Gen's got sales under control. Benko says things have never been smoother. The kids miss you."

"I miss them a lot. Give them big hugs. You, too, honey."

"Take care of yourself, Charlie. Bye."

*She didn't say she missed you. When's the last time she really kissed you?*

I think she half-missed me and was half-glad to have some time alone. Nora was the smartest woman I ever knew. She had the vocabulary of a college English professor and she could talk numbers and taxes well enough to impress my accountant. She was my board of directors for the company, and any of my business associates who met her always told me that I was lucky to have such a business partner. But when it came to marriage, is she smart? I don't think so. Am I smart? No way.

Deborah, the infallible therapist, said one of the 'spousal parties' is the change agent and one is the stabilizer. Nora's definitely the change agent for our relationship. I didn't have the time or the energy for that. I put all my change agency into running a business and trying to make money so I practice *wu wei* with my wife. Non-action. Let if flow.

Except, lately, I tiptoed around Nora—I could never give her quite what she wanted. She's the one who should have felt guilty. I didn't have an affair in public like she did with her painting teacher. Somehow she blamed me for her fling, and I believed her, to a degree. If I'd had time to give her all the attention she said she needed, I'd never get any work done. She and I went over it a hundred times: She slept with the guy because he made her feel special, and I didn't. Have we been married too long? I've never stopped loving her, though.

She pissed me off so much I thought about leaving, but I'd never let her know how much it hurt me that she slept with that goose-necked Picasso wannabe. She'll never learn that he left town a month after I found out about her and him because I called in a private eye from Syracuse who got some nice shots of him with two other women. I should have shown them around, but I'd never bring shame into my family by exposing Nora's idiocy.

I called him up, told him to meet me for lunch. He sat down and I laid the pictures out in front of him on the tablecloth, and said, "You've got 24 hours to lose yourself."

"What are you talking about? This is bullshit."

I glared at him with my narrowest Jack Nicholson eyes and laughed. I never felt better than when I saw the expression on his face as he threw down a twenty to pay for my lunch and ran to his car.

Therapy made it clear that I didn't want to leave Nora and she didn't want to leave me for him. Anybody can give into temptation, and I don't have a double standard here.

She'd said I neglected her soul but I still have no idea what she means. Maybe she'd feel I cared for her soul if I asked her to get more involved in the day-to-day business. She'd share the angst in the moment, rather than listening to my second-hand tales, which always sounded like griping. She already worked with Genevieve whenever she wanted to and she was in charge of the company's Human Resources. I hung her art in the office and we had a big celebration when she sold her first painting to the woman Genevieve introduced her to.

When I said that her soul would feel a lot more taken care of if she worried less about it, she screamed at me, "What about you? I know you fuck around on all those sales trips."

I screamed back, "The hell I do. I've had plenty of chances, but I don't. I take our marriage seriously."

She broke down when I said that and she pushed herself out of her chair across the therapist's office and gave me a huge hug.

I said, "Take the opposite of what you feel now. That's how I feel about you fucking around."

She snapped her head back and raised her palm, but she didn't strike. She's a passionate woman and I love her for it but how long I put up with her passion for somebody else is another story.

Maybe if I'd forgiven her in the spring after the painter split town and if Nora told me how sorry she was, I'd never have noticed Becky, much less slept with her. I was so angry with her for having an affair, I guess I tried to get even with her.

***

Last winter, worn out from our huge Year of the Monkey sales push, enervated but innocent of any inkling that death and doom waited only a few months ahead, Nora and I decided to reward ourselves with a Caribbean vacation. Deborah, the know-it-all therapist, encouraged us to go so we reserved two weeks in a small resort in the Dominican Republic.

Four days after we arrived, I came down with food poisoning or mild sunstroke. Whatever it was laid me low and kept me in bed for a week where I sweat through the sheets every afternoon. I tried swimming at dusk, but my legs dragged across the sand to the shore where I would lay, half-submerged in crystalline eighty-plus degree water, shivering.

At first, Nora was angry with me. "Why didn't you wear that beautiful straw hat I bought you? You don't have to prove you're Tarzan."

"Hey."

"You don't. You didn't have to devour those mangoes without washing them, either. Or papayas."

"Maybe it was the lettuce at the resort salad bar." I had no strength to fight with her.

"I ate the lettuce. I'm fine. You wanted this trip. Now you're ruining it."

I couldn't handle her energy level. I wasn't going to take the blame for her disappointment, so I said, "You go have fun, for both of us."

She did.

I stayed in the little room, lying on the bathroom floor in front of the fan, vomiting, drinking gallons of bottled water, crawling in and out of soggy sheets, sleeping fifteen hours a day while Nora rode horses, snorkeled, sailed, learned the merengue, and turned as brown as the natives.

She rejuvenated herself into the gorgeous babe she was when I first met her, but I had no libido, so I couldn't appreciate her the way she deserved, or the way I deserved. For a whole week my skin prickled whenever she touched me. I wanted to go home before we'd used half our reservation, but I kept quiet.

With my first breath of frigid air when we got off the plane at home, a thrill ran through me as if I'd just won a marathon or deposited a million dollars in the bank. I couldn't believe how the snow heaped along the runway excited and welcomed me.

Nora and I might have traveled to two different places— she to a tropical paradise where she became bronzed and beautiful, me to an indoor diet clinic where I lost ten pounds I didn't need to lose and stayed pale as a worm.

When we discussed our experience with Deborah, I suspected that Nora enjoyed the heat in ways I didn't want to think about. She laughed about how warm and friendly the people were and how one of the guys dived fifty feet down without oxygen to pluck off a branch of elkhorn coral for her.

When she told Deborah about the merengue dances and mambos the resort held every night and the Spanish she'd learned, her voice crackled with excitement. I may have been

paranoid, or jealous, but I asked her why she was so enthusias-
tic when she talked about the trip with Deborah.

"Charlie, sweetie, I had a great time. Thank you for taking
me." "We took ourselves," I grumbled.

"I didn't want to upset you anymore than you were."

That sounded true enough, and I appreciated her sensitivity. I told her how glad I was that she had so much fun. I admitted that she did check on me often when I was sick, brought me
water, washed the mangoes and lettuces when I could eat them,
and brought me beer from the cabaña when I could drink it.

But a couple of weeks after we returned, Nora brought up
the subject of "restructuring our relationship."

Now I got mad. "What the hell do you mean?" I shouted.
My voice was so loud that I glanced at Deborah to make sure
I was playing by therapy rules. She just nodded her head, en-
couraging me.

Nora said she just didn't know for sure that monogamy was
always good for every couple.

"You go down that road," I said, "you go alone. I'm not interested. Who are you fucking now?"

"I'm not fucking anybody! I just think we should open up
the way we think about marriage. Be mature about it. It doesn't
have to mean sleeping with other people."

Jesus, I thought. She's been reading those New Age books
about opening up our thinking about everything like we were
old blankets that needed airing out.

"You guys are really getting somewhere, Charlie. Nora is
still playing her role as your change agent, while you're opting
for stability, keeping your marriage anchored. You're talking
about things together that will really take you deep. Everything
is right on track."

*You got a one-way ticket to Cuckoldville. Your therapist sounds like
Nora's shill.*

But that night, Nora and I made the fiercest love we'd
made for years, since before Chuckie was born. We agreed as

we drifted off to sleep that maybe this shouting and fighting in therapy was working after all.

***

Lying there nearly comatose in the Delight Hotel, as I meditated on the state of my marriage, a state I might not long reside in, I tried to recall that night with Nora. I felt a little sputtering of desire, but my back hurt too much to jerk off, so I lay there steeping in fantasies of what might have been, wishing my aching body would dissolve in the tropical drizzle.

***

I was chewing the ice of my third Johnny Black of the night, courtesy of the Delight Hotel or Hotel Delight, feeling numb and drowsy when the room phone rang. Eleven thirty, already a half hour past my Taipei bedtime. I hoped it was Nora again, because I doubted I could have a rational conversation with anybody else.

"Hello Charlie? Charlie Greer?"

My God, what did he want? "Aaron. You found me."

"Not too hard. Tried three times then got smart. Called the international operator and she put me right through."

"What can I do for you, Aaron? I was almost asleep."

"Oh, what is it, yeah, middle of the night over there. How's the jet lag?"

"Bad. I hurt my back. All I do is lay around my room."

"Sorry about that. Try ibuprofen. Keeps the swelling down and chases the bad chemicals away. Doc Wallace told me about it." "That's what I'm doing."

"This call's expensive so I'll get right to it. I'd Skype but I don't have time right now."

"That's all right, Aaron. I'd have to turn on my iPad."

"Sure. No problem." He paused.

I heard him take a deep breath.

"Two things. Somebody says they saw your car in the Mac-Daniel neighborhood."

I jerked straight up in bed with no pain. "What do you mean? When? I was in the neighborhood sometime. I've been in every neighborhood. Clement's small."

"A couple times. The night of the murder and a week or so before."

"Don't know how it could be, Aaron. My Jeep's not the only one in town."

"They said it was white like yours."

"So what? Lotsa white SUVs—"

"Said the driver looked just like you."

I let that sink in while I got out of bed to pace. My back spasmed and I went to my knees. I choked off my groan. "Not much evidence," I gasped, "Anybody could be driving."

"Well, maybe. The other was your rig was at Brownwell's Supermarket, two, three times. Got your license plate—TO-FU4U."

"Remember I told you about my job? I visit stores to see how our tofu is selling? I also do a lot of the family shopping. Brownwell's locally owned and I support local businesses. Keep our cash in our town."

"You're a local hero, Charlie. Like the article in the paper said last year."

His praise sounded sarcastic, but I couldn't tell for sure. My B.S. detectors had almost shut down for the night under the cozy blanket of booze.

*The booze shut your radar down. Turn it on or Buhrman will top you with a thorny crown.*

"Wait a minute, Aaron. I gotta get comfortable." I had to lie down on the bed with my legs propped on a pillow. "I'm set." Buhrman resumed. "The other thing ..."

I didn't like it when he paused so long.

"Your fingerprint. We got it off a glass in the dead woman's place."

Shit. How did he do that? He had me in her house, drinking something. Why didn't she wash the dishes any better? I thought quickly about that last night. I didn't go inside then or anytime in the previous week. The print must be old.

"Could only be one thing," I said, adopting my co-investigator's ploy as well as I could. "'Member I told you I took her home from the comp'ny party? Musta had a glass a water or sum thin."

"You drinking, Charlie?"

"Had a few tonight. For the pain. Works good with the naproxen." I chuckled and he laughed, too.

"Yeah, well, maybe that explains it. You had a glass of water, you say?"

"I was the designated driver at the party, Aaron. Ask the workers. Wasn't about to drink anything else with an employee. 'Specially a woman late at night."

"Okay."

"Don't make more of this than there is. Bet you got fingerprints from two dozen people who work at the factory."

"Good guess. Twenty-seven. Talking to 'em all."

"Lotta work, Aaron. For an accident."

"Gotta go with my gut, Charlie."

"Hope the taxpayers don't run out of money paying for your gut, Aaron, I gotta go to sleep. Anything else?"

"No. Thanks for your help. Have a good trip. Make sure you come back."

I set the receiver down and threw my arms out across the bed. That dog. Good thing I already admitted I'd gone to her house, the one time that was public knowledge anyway. Surprising, he bagged my Jeep in Brownwell's parking lot. Twenty-seven sets of prints. That must have been a hell of a birthday party.

I tossed down the rest of my drink and lay in the dim light with my eyes open. He really meant it when he said he hoped my back got better. I wasn't the bad guy, yet.

***

The next morning, I rolled out of bed, clear in my head, with back pains a little dulled. I'd handled the call from Buhrman without giving away my shock. Now he'd keep himself busy interviewing the twenty-seven others for the rest of my trip, so I was free of him for a while.

After lying around until afternoon and finishing off a packet of Advil, I dragged myself downstairs and outside, and limped around Taipei's smoky streets, searching for a drugstore and more painkillers. Nobody had ibuprofen or even aspirin.

I finally found a pharmacy where I found a bottle of naproxen. I swallowed a handful of pills, then, hobbling and stopping every few steps, I trekked beyond the hotel's immediate neighborhood into a perpetual construction zone. Wrecking balls pounded incessantly against brown concrete buildings of the same size and shape as nearby buildings that seemed to rise, cloning the ruined ones as soon as they collapsed. Under the foreboding sky clogged with dust, Taipei reminded me of the black and white photos I'd seen of bombed-out Warsaw after the Second World War.

I'd come to Taipei with the romantic delusion that I'd be welcomed into a thriving modern metropolis. I expect it to be built with the refined esthetic sense of the noble refugees determined to preserve the old empire in their Taiwan island refuge. I expected to have discussions with natives about Chinese history, Mao and his place in history, their prosperous manufacturing economy, the electronic age that made them rich.

Instead of educated, informed citizens engaging me in dialogues, the din of thousands of mopeds and motor scooters rip-sawed at my eardrums and their acrid exhausts seared my eyes and nasal tissues. I retched and coughed. Finally, I stopped a pedestrian and pointed to the surgical mask he wore. He said something and rushed on so I tied my handkerchief around my face like a rustler in the movies. With my lungs somewhat protected, I relaxed a little.

Around me, manic Taipeians ignored the pollution, racing around the streets, bargaining incessantly, creating the next million dollars per hour of export surplus to the US. My businessman's calculating mind began to despair. How my sweet little American Tofu company could ever compete with the voracious twenty four seven commercial spirit of the Taiwan Tiger, the spirit that guided Meng, I couldn't conceive.

On every block, a Buddhist supplies store sold incense, herbs, cloth, prayer sheets, and other things I couldn't identify. I bought a small pack of prayer papers, delicate tan rice paper with a gold square in the center that fit into a shirt pocket—convenient replacements for bloody pig or chicken sacrifices.

After watching the locals make their offerings to Buddha, I stood outside the store and lit a few of the prayer papers over an urn in front of the store, placed on the sidewalk for the customers who had burning needs to get Buddha's attention.

Like the other devotees, I held the flaming papers while they vaporized in my fingers until the ash dropped into the urn. The smoke drifted up, mingling with the toxic motor scooter fog and the construction dust and the oily tropical mist, finding its way right into Buddha's nose.

That was probably the original purpose of the fire sacrifice— tickle the Buddha's nose with smoke and make him sneeze squalls of rain onto the rice fields.

As I headed toward the Delight and the calm of my room, I passed dozens of aromatic food carts lining the narrow alleys abutting the main shopping street. Barbecued meat and the saucy noodles and exotic fruits tempted my curiosity more than my appetite. Before I came to Taiwan, I'd met an American who lived in Taipei for two years, returned to the States, then six months later, she lost all her hair.

"Parasites," she told me. "I ate everything."

Determined to keep my hair as long as I could, I decided not to pick from the carts except for some kai, a crimson apple-shaped pear. With fantasies of importing the *kai* by the container load to feed obese Americans a crisp and juicy health snack, I carried several to my room to wash before I ate. Except for carton after carton of guava juice I picked up in little shops, I ate all my meals in the restaurants around the hotel or in my room.

That night, as I nibbled some deep-fried pork and fish combination with seaweed-flavored rice and sampled a local beer, I listened to the English-language radio station playing classical music. The music gave me a shudder of familiarity—it could have been WRUR in Rochester—and my mind cleared.

As I sat there half a world away from Clement, I saw that ever since that night I'd taken on the victim mentality.

Backtracking from the Chief, fearing his next phone call, my mind racing from calculating the consequences of every lie to imagining my future wandering the homeless streets as a smelly ex-con.

Terrified of how my family and friends would scorn me, how my whole life, all my work, was futile—if I got caught. More than my fear, I was fed up with being on the defensive. I hadn't become a success by waiting around for prosperity to tap me on the shoulder when I wasn't looking.

I ordered up a pot of Oolong tea and pulled out my laptop. I started writing the "What if" exercise I'd learned at one of the Young Presidents weekend seminars. What if I had a million dollars? What if Buhrman went away? What if I could get the whole New York State school system to buy tofu? What if the President declared October is National Tofu Month? What if scientists found that tofu not only prevented cancer but it made you feel and act ten years younger? What if I came back from Taiwan as the Tofu Tiger? What if Shu Ling invited me to live with her in New York? What if Shu Ling and I took a yearlong trip around the world?

*What if the Chief finds out the truth? Now's the time to plan your escape route.*

I felt regenerated and relaxed after I finished that fantasy tripping—my life was an atlas of open roads, not a maze of dead ends. Even after three cups of tea, I fell asleep and slept nine hours without getting up once.

***

I woke up the next morning with an erection in my lap and the words "Soy to the World" singing in my ears, tickling like Shu Ling's tongue, and I laughed out loud.

I headed for the shower and as I stood under the water, I noticed my back was free of pain. I bent sideways and forwards and backwards and almost had a full-range swivel. I started singing out 'Soy to the World .'

"Soy to the World, The beans have come, Let earth receive her curd."

I toweled off, musing about the lyrics—Becky said curds reminded her of Little Red Riding Hood. She got her fairy tales mixed up, but I never said anything.

I realized why I was in Taipei with no distractions until Meng returned from the south—I had the time and now the energy, at last, to create the greatest tofu promotion ever: "Soy to the World". We'd launch it with the next Chinese New Year. What better time to make a huge racket than at the dawn of the upcoming Year of the Rooster?

Lots of people ate soy these days—every supermarket had dozens of soy meats, soy cheeses, soymilks, soy this, soy that. But really, it was the same old gang that supported the industry: women worried about menopause and the natural foods mavens. They made up a tiny portion of the big picture. Soy to the World would create a whole new consciousness among the pizza gobblers, the grillmeisters, and the ninety eight percent who think "toad food" and their stomachs cramp.

All morning I paced around the room, dictating ideas into my phone. Here was the perfect chance to practice the 'Hundredth Monkey' marketing theory. Becky told me about it. An-thropologists showed that once monkeys start washing their potatoes on a remote island, when that fateful hundredth monkey scrubbed his spuds, every monkey in the world spontane-ously washed their potatoes. Only my monkeys were people and my potatoes were cakes of tofu.

That night I'll call Gen and Nora and enlist them. They'd be monkeys two and three on the way to the hundred. We'd call it 'The Hundred Monkeys Campaign.' On second thought, Soy to the World had all the punch we needed and not half the silliness monkeys would bring to it.

I made my to-do list.

> —Get everyone on board Soy to the World Express
> —Call trademark attorney. Get the ball rolling on registration
> —Bring in Rick and team from ad agency
> —Start P.R. campaign to swamp the media
> —Email , Facebook friends, twitter customers, suppliers, consumers
> —Get everyone on board the Soy to the World Express
> —Build up head of steam—no company can touch us—Canadian , Californian , Taiwanese, nobody!!!!

While writing, I realized a major side benefit . We'd have so much activity around the plant and I'd be so totally dedicated to STTW, I wouldn't worry about Buhrman. All he would see was a hard-working leader out to do the best he could for his company. Would a likely murderer throw himself into creative work like this? No, he'd worry about his secrets, get depressed, cover up his lies, sneak away if he could. I felt like Becky was an angel hovering nearby guiding me.

I faxed, emailed, and called everyone I could reach that night and the next. In three days, I broadcast the idea to every soy producer listed in the Soybean Blue Book, the industry bible. I wanted insider feedback and Genevieve's touch on the idea before we publicized it on our website, blog, facebook or on our packaging and fifty more ways. Before long, American Tofu would be the lead marketer of soy foods in the world.

After my third super-productive day of work on Soy to the World, I got a call from William Woo Ai, Meng's English-speaking Taipei liaison. Eager to speak with a friendly person, I told him about my back problem, the immense amount of work I'd accomplished and how, now, I was ready to meet some natives.

"We'll take care of you, Charlie. I have a lovely evening arranged for you. A nice massage, some local people?"

"Sounds great. Can you bring me some naproxen? I ran out of mine." I anticipated an excellent acupressure massage. I'd heard about the Chinese tradition of training blind people to become masseurs and masseuses.

"I'll pick you up tonight, Charlie."

I climbed into the taxi with William as the muggy city twilight deepened. Behind windows closed against the clouds of exhaust smoke, shutting out the 90-percent humidity and 90-degree temperature, we launched into a night aflame with pink and chartreuse bouncing off a low sky. The cab bumped down narrow cobbled streets designed and built for buggies and motor scooters. Metallic blue and orange neon, glaring and flashing lights and signs screamed for attention from a disinterested crowd.

We turned off the main road into a residential area. Crowds bumped continually against the car. At stoplights people of all ages leaned casually against it while they held conversations, as if we'd rolled into their living rooms, a kind of mobile couch.

As we inched our way through the crowd, the people banged the hood or the trunk and waved through the side windows at me in some kind of ritual. I held my back as still as I could as the taxi swerved to avoid bikes, mopeds, pedestrians. Dozens of delivery trucks jammed the street.

"The stores stay open all night," William said. "Everybody has lots of money and not enough to buy."

I was glad there were only twenty million Taiwanese in the world economy. I had a vision of the twenty-second century, when China dominated the overpopulated world with its noise and smog and hustle, I was glad I wouldn't be around. We rode in silence until the car pulled into a large courtyard where it stopped and William climbed out.

"I have an early meeting, Charlie. Lin will take care of everything," he said, nodding toward the driver. "I'll call you in the morning."

I called out the window to him. "William, where am I going?" "Lin knows, Charlie. Have a good time." He waved and disappeared into a storefront.

*The driver's a thug. You shoulda stayed in and taken more drugs.*

Exhaustion settled into my spirit. I'd been working long hours and I was too weak to try to control the situation. I'd just have to let happen whatever came next. I closed my eyes, to escape the lights and sounds of the city.

The car stopped on a wide street in front of a long red awning that stretched from a building out to the street. Two young men wearing black pants and starched white shirts approached the cab. Lin barked at them, tossed one the car keys, while the other opened my door quickly.

I climbed out, curious now, and we trailed the men up wide stairs carpeted in the same reddish-gray color as the awning. The rug led into a lobby where six or seven young women wearing pink skirts and peach-colored blouses lounged on plastic lawn chairs. Illuminated by tiny spotlights, three-foot tall palm trees grew out of pots placed along the walls. Responding to Lin's signal, several young women rose from their chairs and followed him down some stairs.

I waited, examining the surroundings, the first semi-private building I'd been inside in Taipei. Its old carpet was worn to the woof in spots and the rouge and black lobby walls were chipped. Some older women sitting at the bar smiled and waved their down-turned hands at me, urging me to catch up with Lin.

As I descended the stairs to the basement, a cloying bitter smell rose up like cleaning fluid or insecticide. At the bottom, I turned into a narrow hall where several doors lined the corridor. Grinning, Lin pointed to an open door and signed to go in. He pointed at his watch and at the chair behind me. I supposed he meant he'd wait there.

A wrinkled leather recliner filled most of the wood-paneled cubicle. Facing the chair, a fluorescent tube shone over a mirror at the end of the room, lighting the tiny room with chilly reflections. I climbed into the chair and lay back, expecting the masseuse to arrive any minute.

A girl no older than fifteen came in wearing the same peach and pink outfit as the women upstairs. Maybe she was older. I can't tell how old or young Chinese are.

She carried a mug of steaming water, a tea bag, and a lemon. Setting the cup down, she inserted the tea bag, and turned to me.

She smiled weakly, pointing her pinkie finger to my shoes and belt. I got up and deposited my shoes next to the wall and dropped back into the chair.

Groans and coughs came from the other cubicles. My little masseuse ignored the sounds and shook her finger at me, pointing to my belt again. She turned away, reaching into one of the drawers near the mirror.

When she faced me again, she held a large jar of Vaseline in one hand and a towel in the other. She aimed at my crotch, while she circled her fingers and wagged them up and down in the universal jerk-off motion.

*Here it is, playtime for the Chinese business mob. You're in a "barber-shop," where guys come for a hand job.*

I stared at the girl, unsure what to do. She shrugged her shoulders and set the Vaseline jar on a table beside the chair. She reached for my belt and began to unbuckle it. I'd tightened it to the last notch because it supported my sore back, so she had to concentrate on loosening the tine from the hole, yanking it so hard my back spasmed and I cringed.

She ignored my flinching and focused on her task. Finally, she pulled the buckle free and quickly unbuttoned the top button and with a flourish of her wrist, unzipped my pants. She stuck her little hand into my boxers, sliding it further in.

Her fingers felt like cold Jell-O slipping down my belly. My penis had shrunk and retreated deep between my thighs. As she probed, her fingernails nicked my scrotum and I jerked. She stopped moving, anticipating more tremors from me. I wiggled and tilted my pelvis a little so she could have freer access.

After slithering her hand in and out of my pubic hair and across my thighs, she finally found my penis in its burrow, pinched it, and tugged it out of its hiding place. She removed her hand from my shorts and patted my penis through the cloth.

Standing beside me and reaching across my body with one hand, she grabbed the waist of my pants in both hands and began to wrestle them down over my hips.

The girl hadn't shown me her eyes since she first came into the room. She lowered her head almost to my chest and heaved, trying to lift my hips up and pull the pants down at the same time. I weighed at least twice as much as her, and must have felt like dead weight. I couldn't help her because whenever I tried to raise my butt off the chair, my back screamed.

She tugged for at least a minute without moving the pants over my hip bones. She glanced at me, bent her elbows and tugged a couple of more times and she snatched them down to my knees, exposing my legs to the air-conditioning blowing down from the ceiling. Goose bumps embossed my thighs.

The girl frowned and pointed at my boxers that lay across my pelvis like a sagging veil. She gestured for me to finish the job of exposing my parts and turned to the table.

Chilly breeze from the ceiling poured over my exposed middle. I shivered. I wanted a blanket. She could do what she wanted to me, but if I wasn't warm, I wouldn't have any fun. I turned in the chair and retrieved my jacket. Once I laid it on my stomach, I felt a lot better.

The girl, busy at the table, ignored me and squeezed the lemon into the tea cup. Facing the wall, with back to me, she lifted the cup and sipped. She bent over the table again.

As I wriggled out of my underpants, I studied her in the mirror in front of me. I watched her in profile as she pulled on a pair of surgical gloves. She stabbed her fingers into the Vaseline jar, raked a gob of grease into her palm, and turned to me.

I had my hands on my underpants with my knees bent up.

I let them go and pointed to the gloves. She shook her head up and down several times and reached for my jones. It had shriveled even further into a tiny question mark in my lap.

*Check out the gloves. She's gonna give you Latex love.*

I considered the gloves and thought "AIDS."

The whole scene had mesmerized me so much I forgot about AIDS. The girl probably had it. It's rampant in Asia. The only prostitutes that don't have it are the virgins. Those Japanese businessmen who travel around Thailand and Taiwan on the sex tours cruising for young girls, they must have a death wish. I didn't. Gloves or no gloves. Besides, the image of rubber gloves pumping my cock brought a giggle to my throat. I almost laughed out loud.

Shaking my head and grinning, I gripped her empty hand in both of mine and snapped the wrist band of the rubber glove. She stiffened and stared at me wide-eyed. I gesticulated with the universal hands-down, facial disgust "No" sign.

Leaving her cool gloved hand in mine, she just as vehemently rocked her head up and down.

I whipped my head back and forth and grabbed her other hand. I felt about as turned on as if I were naked in the dentist's office with the drill buzzing in my mouth. If that girl touched me with those icy rubber gloves, my penis would shrivel to the size of a toothpick.

As she tried to free her hands from mine, a clot of icy Vaseline dripped onto my navel. I let her go. With her hands in mid-air, she stood inert, almost catatonic, staring at me with her fine lips frozen into a maroon Cheerio.

My nose came to the rescue. The air conditioning blew a stink of rancid fried food laced with a pungent scent of Lysol across my face and I sneezed sharply. The girl jumped back, bumping against the wall. Rhythmic banging noises came from outside my cubicle.

I toweled the grease off my stomach and handed it to the girl. I shrugged my shoulders, and slid down out of the chair.

My back balked as I straightened up, but I managed to pull my pants up without staggering.

As I buckled my belt and began to stand up, the girl bit her lips and pushed me back into the chair with her Vaselined glove. I said "No!" and she bolted, backing into the corner.

I smiled, groaned, got to my feet. I kept shaking my head vigorously at her and saying "No." She kept shaking her head "Yes," and I kept shaking mine "No."

She ran out of the room, banging the door.

After fumbling with my shoelaces I finally tied them. Creaking my stiff back straight, I pulled out my wallet and left an American twenty-dollar bill on the seat of the chair and I made my way into the hallway.

Lin burst out of the room next to mine, shoeless, tucking his shirt into his pants, in a panic. Several doors opened and women wearing the peach blouses peeked out of every one.

I laughed and pointed to a chair in the adjoining hallway. With both hands, I signed to him to go back into his room. I showed him that I'd wait. He understood and turned around, relief on his face.

I discovered the source of the rhythmic banging and it wasn't fucking. In a little room beside the cubicles, a woman stuffed a soggy pile of hand-job cloths into a washing machine while beside her, an upright laundromat-style dryer rotated, thumping its pale load

I made my way upstairs where one of the women served me a pink guava drink. In about five minutes, Lin rushed upstairs, said something gruff to the women, and, clutching my arm, pulled me outside. The taxi hurtled out of the unlit side street into the light in front of the barbershop. I climbed into the back seat as Lin zoomed into the night.

Back in my hotel, in the scalding shower, I laughed and laughed, feeling better than ever since I arrived in Taipei. Healing through humor, I thought.

Meng called the next morning. "How are you, Charlie? Enjoying Taipei?"

I told him about my back and the hilarious mistake Woo Ai had made. "She was going to give me a massage all right. I was expecting something a little different. For my back." I chuckled. "All she wanted to do was my front."

"Many of my American friends enjoy nice Taipei haircuts, Charlie," Meng said seriously. "They're quite safe. I thought you knew about them. I'm sorry you didn't have a good time."

"I had a good time, Meng. Feel a lot better. I just didn't need a haircut."

"Perhaps because you're married?"

"I'm trying to stay married, Meng. But that's not why. I just didn't feel like it. It surprised me, I guess."

"Maybe some other time, Charlie?"

"I don't think so, Meng. That place stunk."

*Watch your mouth, Greer. Meng's calling the shots here.*

I suddenly understood that he'd set up the hand job for me. He might even have chosen the barbershop because it was AIDS-free. He said it was "safe." I stuck my foot deeper in. "I mean, Lysol. They used some heavy disinfectant to wash the cloths. The chairs were in the basement. Lousy ventilation. I could barely breathe."

"Sorry, Charlie. Too bad it smelled. You could have had a good Chinese time."

I reversed as fast as I could. "It wasn't all that bad, Meng. Must have been my back. You know how sometimes you have a pain in one place and it affects some other part?"

"I see. Well, that must be it, Charlie."

"Meng, one more thing. I've been working on Soy to the World. I have some great ideas I'd like to run by you. This will be the most fantastic publicity ever to hit tofu."

"No doubt it will. You have brilliant thoughts and strategies. Why don't we talk about it back in the States."

Was he brushing me off? "It's pretty hot in my mind right now, Meng. If we—"

"You're working too hard, Charlie. Too much thinking can ignite your head. Like you say, one part of our body can cause problems elsewhere. Too much heat here, not enough over there."

"Uh, yes. I know what you mean. Gotta keep things in balance."

"I agree. Now, relax and we'll work really hard when we get home. What do you say?"

"Thanks, Meng."

"William will be in touch with you in the morning. Good bye, Charlie."

I hung up and sank onto my bed.

I like all kinds of sex. But not by some child wearing cold greasy plastic gloves in a stinking hotel basement.

*You should be smarter. You won't get another chance later.*

I did what I did and it's done.

*He'll never be your partner now. He won't trust you. You rejected his gift. Boo hoo.*

Did I just blow the chance to become one of the guys the Chinese way? I couldn't do it any other way. Sometimes you just have to play it loose and let the chips fall where they may.

# Chapter Eight

## *Genevieve*

# THE CHIEF'S INTIMATIONS

Nora and I met almost daily to organize the details of the trust fund for the MacDaniel children. She handled the legal and financial details while I raised money from customers and local business groups. Charlie had managed to raise thirty thousand dollars from his peers in the industry, so the MacDaniel orphans had a solid start on their college education.

After Charlie left for Taiwan, Nora invited me to breakfast. "Let's go to Lazy Meadows over in Whitfield," she said. "I feel like splurging on their Northern Spy apple pancakes."

"And getting out of town?" I asked.

"We can talk," she said. "Nobody knows us there."

Nora barely touched her pancakes. I'd never eaten them before and they tasted so good I offered to help.

"Take them," she said. "I haven't had much appetite lately."

"I can see it in your face. You should sleep more, Nora."

"The Chief asked me to come to his office to talk with him so I went to the city hall. I'd never been inside a police station before." "Me either."

"It gave me the creeps. Hospital green walls, cold overhead lights, black filing cabinets everywhere. He kept it neat, I'll say that for him. He had a couple of yellowing ivies and some spider plants on the windowsills, but once I stepped inside the door, I felt like I should confess."

"Confess *what*? What could he want with *you*?"

"He said he had to talk with everybody from the company. I thought he'd ask about our personnel records, maybe he found a mistake. With so many forms, who can expect our staff to cross every t?"

Nora sat still while she spoke, her lips barely moving, her fingers wrapped around her teacup but never lifting it. I didn't know if she was scared or mad.

"Anyway, he congratulated me on the records. 'Very nice company, Mrs. Greer. You seem to have everything in order. People like working there. It's clean. Except that okaroka out back.'"

"Okaroka?" I said.

Furrowing her forehead, Nora smiled without showing her teeth. "He meant okara. You know how it smells, especially in hot weather." She went on. "He wanted to talk about me and Charlie. He said he'd heard from a little birdie that a former friend of mine had left town suddenly and Charlie was the reason for it. When he asked, 'Was that true?' I stood up and said, 'Leave my relationship out of this. You have no right to pry into my and my husband's personal life.' I was pissed."

Nora tapped the table with one hand while she twirled her fingers in her hair with the other. I reached over and covered her hand with mine. She let her hair go and grasped my hand.

"I would be, too. That Chief has no boundaries. You'd think he'd show a little respect to you, after all you've done for the Mac-Daniel kids."

Nora sipped her tea and called the waitress over to ask for more hot water. Crisp sunlight poured through the restaurant's front window. But around my legs, the room held its chill. Nora stared out the front window.

Nora thanked the waitress and turned her eyes back to me. "My anger was an act. I don't know how I pulled it off. My heart was pounding and instead of falling apart, I got mad. The way he'd been sticking his nose in everybody's business, y'know. Did he get to you yet?"

"Not yet," I said.

"He will. I asked him if I needed an attorney and he said no. I sat down and said I wouldn't think so. But right then, y'know, I decided to call Fred Fierst. Charie told me I should if I needed help while he was in Taiwan."

"Good idea," I said.

Nora continued, tapping the table again with her free fingers. "Then Buhrman said, 'Mrs. Greer, this is just as hard for me.' He looked a little embarrassed, rosy in his cheeks and around his collar. But he'd tied his tie so tight, it could have caused the red. Maybe he was faking like me, y'know."

I nodded.

"I asked him to just call me Nora. He seemed relieved and told me I should call him Aaron. 'At the bottom here, Nora, we're just neighbors. Fellow citizens of Clement. I'm doing my job and I hope you understand that.'"

"I can see why you were creeped out. He sounds like he's trying to be bad cop and good cop at the same time."

"It turned out he was all right. I told him Charlie and I had gone through some rough times recently, like any married couple. When he heard that he blurted out, 'Me and Gloria never did.' I said, 'I'm glad you were spared the misery, 'but some people have more pressures in their lives than others.'"

"I don't like this guy," I said.

"Buhrman's a country bumpkin."

"Don't underestimate him," I said.

Nora leaned forward and I followed her into the private space above our cups.

"He was leading up to one question, y'know: Did Charlie have anything to do with Becky?"

"What does he think he's doing?" I said.

"My reaction exactly, but I played it cool. If he involves Charlie in something dicey here, we could all be in trouble. Imagine the press."

"Can't someone stop that bastard?"

"I don't know. Trying that could be worse, because only the guilty object to a careful murder investigation. Like, Catch 22."

The waitress came over to ask if we needed anything else and to clear our plates. I asked for a cup of coffee, something stronger than my peppermint tea.

Nora continued. "I told him Charlie was her boss, and we had three layers of management between him and her. But Charlie's gregarious. He knows all the workers, talks to everybody. It's one of the reasons people like to work for AT. Charlie's available."

"The Chief listens to me and sits back without saying anything, as if he could frighten me with some kind of accusative silence. Of course, I sit back and wait, too. Then he says, 'Charlie claims he didn't know her.'"

Nora sat straight in her chair and crossed her knees.

"So I say, 'I guess he didn't.'" She grinned and said, "He sat there for a minute, kinda staring at me, then he said, 'Thank you, Nora. You've been a big help.' That was it."

"That was it?"

"Well, for him, it was. He tried to cow me once more. When I got up to leave, he said, 'Would you swear to that in court?' I said, 'Sure.  But what are you implying, Chief?' He said, 'Nothing. Nothing. Just following some leads.' Some leads? I said, or some trumped-up witch hunter's charges? I was furious this time."

So the Chief wants to make Charlie a suspect, I thought. But what could he be suspicious of? A woman dies in a factory and the boss is to blame? Maybe, if we had a shoddy business, but we're one of the most respected companies in upstate New York.

"Nora," I said, "we've got a crazy man wearing the police chief's hat."

"Once I got mad, he apologized. He was sorry for offending me. He gets all formal again. 'We're a small town, Mrs. Greer.' *Mrs. Greer!* 'We have to go out 110 percent. We conduct a superior investigation, nothing gets messy with the D. A.' I didn't know what he meant so I asked 'What do you mean?' He said 'Nothing unusual other agencies. The insurance company, the state health and safety board.'

"I heard that and I understood Buhrman immediately. Like I didn't already know. Who's been dealing with them. Me."

"I get it," I said. "We're supposed to cooperate, be passive, while the Chief investigates whoever he wants because he has to prove how competent he is."

"I guess. I'll tell Charlie when we talk tomorrow, but, like, I don't think we can do anything but stay cool."

For a few minutes, Nora and I sat there telling each other how angry we were, how unfair it was, but as we talked, we acknowledged the reality of accident investigations and the huge liabilities insurance companies could have.

As she opened her car door, Nora said, "Don't worry, Gen. The Chief has another month at most to clear this up. Until then, we just take care of business, y'know." She shivered and we hugged each other hard.

I drove back to Clement in a sober mood, feeling trapped in a flood of official distrust that could seep into every aspect of our lives. I was glad I'd been so careful to keep my affair with Benko a secret. I felt no guilt about it, but in the cloud of suspicion hanging over us, I was leery of someone finding out, especially the Chief. Who knows what he would make of it. Nothing good for anybody but him.

# Chapter Nine

## *Charlie*

# BLOOD MEDICINE

*sneezing incense, dripping blood*
*i slid and slipped,*
*gaining face at last*

Twenty-four hours after the barbershop fiasco, Meng sent William to pick me up for our business dinner. I hoped we'd come to some agreement about our future joint ventures. I planned to explain Soy to the World and offer him credit for the idea. I was sure he'd have contacts in Taiwan and China who could launch the campaign in the East and make it truly global.

In gray twilight, William and I drove across the city to Keelung, Taipei's port, arriving at a block of two-story buildings situated across a wide road from several piers. No signs advertised a restaurant and the windows of the buildings were smudged with grease and soot. Before we entered, we watched dozens of cranes drag containers off the cargo ships and set them down on the piers. Under blinding lights posted along the docks, giant forklifts muscled the containers onto trucks that carted them toward us and off to whatever voracious Taiwan business needed more supplies.

"C'mon," Woo said, opening a heavy steel door. We climbed greasy concrete steps up a hallway lit with a few incandescent bulbs. For a second, I wondered if I was safe, but when I heard laughing coming from a room at the head of the stairs, I relaxed.

Meng stood up to greet me from behind a row of red and black-lacquered carvings of dragons and swans perched like familiars on pedestals in front of the table. The burnished belly of a two-foot tall "Happy Buddha" presided over the table from a shelf beside the table, encouraging the diners to enjoy the nirvana of uninhibited appetites.

"Welcome, Charlie," he said as he pumped my hand. "It's been a long time and I apologize again. Have you had a good time in Taipei?"

I was really glad to see Meng. "No problem, Meng. I got a lot done. Can't wait to tell you about it." From the table, one other man, casually dressed as was Meng, smiled and waved at me and lifted his glass. I could see that this was not the time to talk about my debacle last night—the other man must be the key contact Meng promised me, the one who'd make Soy to the World a slam dunk in the Orient.

With its bare yellow walls and high windows encrusted with grime, the small room seemed more like an empty office than a restaurant. I assumed it was converted from warehouse into a private club for harbor bosses. Indirect lighting crowded the room with shadows of the four of us and the statues, muddying the atmosphere around the table.

Meng introduced me to the man, Yi Lan Sun, apologizing also that he spoke no English, and nodded to the empty chair beside him.

I asked Meng if Yi Lan Sun was related to one of my heroes, the ancient Chinese General, Sun Tzu.

He said something to Sun and they both laughed. He turned to me and said, "Good joke, Charlie. Tonight we'll mix business and pleasure."

"Perfect." I was serious about my question, and Meng was host so I'd have to follow his lead, but I wasn't ready to handle too much 'pleasure.' Another barbershop?

A single yellow bloom rising from a crystal vase flirted with us from the center of the table. Yellow, I thought, watching for omens. The Golden Flower. Secret Taoist medical practices. Yellow. The color of the Golden Mean, the Middle Path.

*Don't get high, don't fall low. Wait for Meng to make his move.*

At an invisible signal, a waiter lit the Sterno flame under a stainless and crystal bowl etched with dragons and loaded with sluggish crawfish. As the broth heated up, the crustaceans began swimming in the ginger soup, their antennae waving silent cries for rescue, before drooping in feeble good-byes. We plucked them out of the broth and dipped them in a chilled sweet sauce, sucking the mild-flavored meat from the shells.

Meng called for the dinner. I'd never seen such a collection of seafood gathered onto one table. Crab stuffed into rose petals surrounding a whole baked carp draped with scales of cucumber slices. Assorted stews displayed in large red-lacquered bowls. We sampled three kinds of mussels and snails served in three kinds of shells: zebra-striped snail shells in pungent sweet sauce, tiny white oyster-like shells drenched in seaweed stock, and pink-and-yellowspotted razor-clam shells soaking in a potent alcohol soup.

After I swallowed a few spoonfuls, my nose watered, my head spun, my heart raced. I wondered if I was in some kind of eating contest, or competitive business dinner ritual where they hauled out the loser and pumped his stomach.

Meng sipped his beer and said, "How do you like the bass? Half hour ago it was swimming without a care."

"Delicious. I've never tasted anything like it."

"The chef arrived from Kaohshiung only a year ago. Already he's one of the most popular in Keelung."

Impressive. Meng was more powerful here than I'd imagined. Who else could hire one of the city's most exclusive chefs, for a private party of four, on demand?

I wanted to angle our conversation toward business but I restrained myself since Meng ate and drank in silence. I followed his example, managing to swell my belly until it bulged like the Happy Buddha's. How the Chinese stay so trim, I'll never understand.

"Our business potential is unlimited, Charlie," Meng commented after he ordered tea. "To celebrate our association," he said, as we watched the waiter pour green tea into tiny red cups painted with black dragons. "This tea costs $700.00 per ounce in Taipei. I import it to New York for some friends." He said something to our dinner partners in Chinese, getting a laugh.

I raised my glass and toasted our association. As my business grew,  I said, I'd learned that it would take years and hundreds of thousands of dollars to educate the non-Oriental population of America to eat enough tofu to make me rich. At that point, a few years ago, I found Meng at Hunts Point and he agreed to distribute American Tofu to oriental markets.

The men laughed politely, then Meng set his cup down. "Things are changing, Charlie."

"It's all yin and yang?" I said. "Which way is it going now?"

"I don't know. If I did, would I be in business? I'd be in Hawaii or New Zealand." He laughed. "What about you?"

"I like business. It's something I was born for. My fate."

I risked exposing my personal philosophy to Meng in hopes that I could generate a cross-cultural respect with him based on ethical principles. If we did everything for the almighty buck, frankly, I wouldn't have a chance going against wealthy, powerful people like him. So, my strategy not only had personal meaning for me, but I felt clever as old Sun Tzu, the ancient general, when I used it.

Meng stayed silent. I wondered if he understood me or if he simply ignored my ploy. Instead, he sent the conversation in an unexpected direction. Leaning back in his chair, he said, "My company has recently developed some new markets. The demand has proven substantial, and the profits quite significant. Mr. Sun here and I need a U.S. import partner. That's why you're here."

I blinked. I'd expected to meet someone who would make tofu in Taiwan as one of our partners, or someone to open up the food distribution channels for a brand Meng and I would create. Big profits and high demand sounded wonderful, but

I was a tofu maker and if Meng insisted on my getting into a new type of business, I might have to decline. I was already cash poor from so much tofu growth and importing. I'd need a whole new department. It would cost thousands and take energy away from Soy to the World.

Turning to him, I opened my mouth to ask what we'd import when Meng said, "The real future is bringing China to the West, and I don't mean like poor people's goods in Wal-Mart. We have precious things the Westerners will buy and never ask the price. Perhaps, you can join us."

"Maybe. Let's discuss it. But there's Soy to the World, Meng. It's a great marketing idea and we can make soy the most profitable food anywhere."

*Can't open up to more than one thing at a time? Meng could be offering you the chance of your lifetime.*

"That's your territory, Charlie," he said, raising his hand to signal the waiter. "As for me, I always take new ideas slowly and surely, until I am absolutely positive they work."

"Soy to the World will work, I'm positive. We have to move on it though. Before the competition." Meng accepted a glass from the waiter and glanced at me with a puzzled frown on his face.

Catching on I was acting too stubborn, obviously in my own interest—a lousy negotiation technique—I said, "You're right. Let's talk about it later."

"Thank you, Charlie. Mr. Sun and I appreciate your sensitivity."

Meng called for another round of beers and the waiters brought out some dense cake. Thinking it was chocolate, I cut and chop-sticked a large slice into my mouth and almost spit the sour, rotten taste out. Grabbing my beer, I washed the 'cake' down as gracefully as I could and laid my sticks beside the plate.

"Stinky tofu, Charlie," Meng said, grinning and placing a dime-sized bit on his lips. "It's our special celebration treat. I see it's an acquired taste."

When I moved my tongue to reply, a foul odor seeped into my nostrils and I gagged. "Yes," I gasped. "I can't believe it's tofu." It smelled like two-month old rotten tofu. Which it probably was.

"Guess we'll need some special products for Western markets. We have to please our customers." Meng laughed, and repeated himself to the others, who laughed and wisecracked because all three Chinese guffawed and grinned at me, the bumbling American who thinks he can do business on equal footing with the ancient masters of trade and taste.

When the table quieted except for the sound of a ceiling fan, I said, "What are we going to import? Tea? Fruit?"

Meng translated and William cracked another one-liner that broke up Meng and Sun. Nodding his head, Meng said, "Special fruit, Charlie. Healing fruit."

Woo stood up and lectured and when he finished, Meng laughed loud. "William suggests we call the import business The Special Fruit Company." The others nearly fell off their chairs.

I missed the joke. My hosts held a long serious conversation while I sipped beer, wondering about the novel fruits I'd seen in the street markets. If we could figure out how to ship them quickly and get them onto the shelves before they spoiled, we might have a business in front of us.

I finished my beer and excused myself to go to the men's room. The waiter led me down a hallway to a luxurious apartment with floor-length windows showing the illuminated harbor. He tugged me away from the view and turned around. I headed down a narrow hall toward the bathroom. With a film of dust on its marble tiles and counters, grease blotching the glass doors to a steam bath, stacks of thick white terrycloth towels sagging on slightly rusted metal shelves, I wondered if I was the first person to use the toilet in a long time.

When I returned, Meng and the others stood waiting for me at the open door. "We'll talk more about the imports later,

Charlie. I'm sorry we have to leave you but Mr. Sun and I have to go back to the south tonight. William will drive you home."

Sensing that I disappointed him by my lack of enthusiasm for his fruit-importing venture, I said "The Special Fruit Company sounds like the future, Meng. I'm sure we can design the right system and get the ball rolling. I'm always open to new things, you know. Importing makes a lot of sense."

"Good, Charlie. That's what I like to hear." He said something in Chinese, everybody laughed again, and we all went into the night to our waiting cars. Across the street, orange and maroon trucks and cranes and forklifts glinted under racks of blinding overhead lights, driven by invisible men, unloading imports, loading exports, carrying Taiwan, like the whole of China, into the wealthy, grimy future.

***

I stayed in bed until noon the next morning. My sore back had returned so I downed a few more naproxen and walked to the street markets. I bought a dozen unfamiliar foods, not knowing the difference between a fruit and a vegetable. I planned to show Meng my research when we next met.

At eight that night, the phone rang and William laughed when I said I forgot that he was coming by. I invited him up to my room to have a drink with me before we went out.

William and I greeted each other warmly.

"Call me Woo, Charlie. After dinner last night, we know each other better."

I handed him a glass of Johnny Black, courtesy of the room's wet bar. "Here you go, Woo. Hair of the dog, we say. Gets rid of the hangover."

"Thanks," he said. "Snout of the pig." He raised his glass in a toast.

We sat for a while, saying nothing, letting the whiskey settle in our stomachs. He emptied his glass and covered it when I offered a refill. "Good time last night?"

"Yes. I loved what the chef could do. I'm sorry we couldn't talk more about business though."

"Mr. Meng takes his time."

"I see that. He told me to slow down Soy to the World. Problem is, I can't. He'll understand." I got up and paced. I needed some action, but my backache had relocated down my sacroiliac into my legs. I had to bring up the massage subject again.

"Woo, my back's feeling lousy again. I wonder if you'd make an appointment for me with one of those blind masseurs? The ones the state trains to see with their fingers?" I wanted no confusion about the type of massage I needed.

"Mr. Meng has a better idea," he said. "We believe that all physical problems start in the blood. Without fresh, pure blood, you can't be strong. Mr. Meng needs you to be strong. Tonight, we'll take some blood medicine."

***

A silver Mercedes waited in front of the hotel. Woo told me to lie across the back seat, "to rest your back," while he rode in front with  the driver. The stout car rolled along the pitted streets as gently as a raft floating across a still pond.

Glossy neon light flowed across the windows in greasy rainbow colors. As we crept through the narrow streets toward Old Taipei, I lay drowsing, sunk in leather cushions, relaxed and content.

We stopped abruptly and Woo said over his shoulder, sharply, "Goddam politicians. Let's go, Charlie. We have to walk. Lin will watch the car."

Angry shouts punctuated by firecrackers popping roared into the car as Woo opened the door. People ran by waving flags and banging on trash can lids.

"It's the government. The new generation thinks it's their turn now. The old boys want to show they still get hard-ons."

"We have demonstrations in the States all the time," I said.

He gripped my arm and led me against the current of the crowd. My sense of being a pawn in someone else's game sharpened, but all I could do was play along. I might as well enjoy myself.

We crossed into an open loading lot where dozens of reeking dumpsters lined the walls on four sides of the square. A throng of men milled around in the putrid night, shouting at each other, hip-checking boxes onto pallets, pirouetting out of the way of the smut-blatting motor scooters, all at an earnest commercial pitch. My nostrils twinged as exhaust fumes assaulted my face.

"Trash sorters," Woo said, impervious to the stinking vapors. "When the shops close, they pick through the dumpsters. They sell to Beijing. Very rich men."

A wave of fatigue rolled over me. My watch said midnight. How long had I dozed in the back of the car? I wanted to go back to the hotel and sleep away my growing befuddlement. The scotch had worn off and the pain had climbed from an ache in my lower back to a knife under my shoulder blades.

Taiwan had taken my measure and I was a lot smaller here than I'd ever been back home and I felt no need to prove myself anymore. For a moment, I shocked myself with a stroke of longing to be back in Clement, volleying insinuations back and forth with the Chief, worrying about sales, dealing with the everyday problems that made my mundane business life exciting. Taipei had satisfied my appetite for the exotic and I was ready to bring the taste of the new to America with Soy to the World, at my pace, on my turf, on my terms.

I slowed down to watch the trash sorters, night buzzards who struck it rich from some deal with a government agent, no doubt. Several thin men scrambled in and out of the dumpsters, hollering at each other. An ebony BMW sat sentry in the shadows at the end of the block.

Woo picked up his pace, tugging my arm hard and drawing me out of my reverie. Turning the corner toward a chartreuse glow yawning from the wall, we stepped through an open storefront into a wide, high-ceilinged shop lit by shining neon ideographs. Glistening white tiles rose to meet wall-length mirrors reflecting so much light that most of the dozen or so people in the room wore sunglasses.

I followed Woo to the back of the shop, my leather soles clicking over the terra cotta floor tiles. The shop smelled slightly of rancid fat or old meat, reminding me of a large restaurant kitchen or the butchery in a grocery store. It was set with trestle tables.

I pointed to the many eight-inch long geckoes that perched near the corner between the walls and ceiling. Woo said, "Geckoes. Do you see any flies?"

I shook my head no.

"Geckoes," he said, dismissing further gecko talk.

Seven or eight boisterous men and a few animated women sat at the table talking. A thin bald man called out "New York!" and raised his glass and toasted me. He tossed off his deep purple wine quickly, leapt up on a chair and began chanting at me, pointing to himself, to his image in the wall mirror, and back to me.

Watching him over my shoulder, I closed the distance between Woo and myself, hoping to defuse the drunk by ignoring him. Woo stopped short and I bumped into him. I groaned an apology for my clumsiness.

"Don't pay attention to him," Woo said, dismissing my self-reproach. "There, Big Man's coming to throw him out."

The largest man I'd seen in Taiwan strolled across the room. Standing at least seven feet tall and four feet wide, he wore a black business suit, black shirt, and black headband restraining a shock of silver hair on his basketball-size head.

The giant curled a trunk of an arm around the drunk's neck and lifted him up. The surprised man twitched on the bouncer's hip, gasping and grunting and kicking as the other drinkers laughed at his predicament.

Oblivious to the commotion, Woo stared intently into a large rectangular aquarium from which, I guessed, he'd select a fish for our midnight dinner. I'd had seafood every dinner since we arrived in Taipei and each dish was exquisitely different from the next.

I edged around Woo to stand beside him, watching him as he made up his mind. The aquarium windows were dry and I couldn't see any fish. The tank's shadowy floor gleamed in the room's haze, an emerald and ivory sheen pulsing slowly, sloshing, like brackish water. I detected a sweet, pungent odor wafting out of the tank.

As Woo stared into the aquarium, I raised my eyes. Hundreds of shadowy, flat snake skins were attached to the wall behind the tank, some entwined, some laid over others, the longest of them climbing from floor to dusky ceiling and stretching out over the room, a bas relief of flat scaly vines. The widest and longest pelts hung like woven blankets, died in earthen tans and browns, patterned in diamonds and swirls, artfully connected with repeated crosshatches.

*Exotic. The adventure you wanted. Be cool. Act undaunted.*

I stared into the tank: the 'fish' were living, coiling snakes. The brackish water was snakes oozing over and under each other, warming themselves in the friction of scaly muscle on muscle. A field of lidless eyes sparkled as blunt heads rose and dipped, curved and turned, pausing in the air as if curious about us. The snakes had heads ranging from the size and shape of flattened ping pong balls to full oval turkey eggs.

A short man wearing an orange and blue flowered shirt draped over an ample stomach approached, smiling, speaking rapidly as he waved his arm over the tank. He reached in, brushing aside several nodding heads. He rummaged through the writhing mound like someone sorting wet laundry.

Woo barked at the man as he lifted a snake, dangling it in front of my face while letting its tail brush back and forth on the floor. I braced myself, waiting for a clue from Woo. I didn't want to make another barbershop blunder.

The man quickly tossed the snake back and bowed to Woo, glancing sideways at me. He signaled for us to follow him. We passed a large cage holding four small monkeys. I stopped Woo to ask about them.

"What are these guys doing here?"

He was so intent on following the tropical shirt, he didn't know what I meant, so I pointed.

"Oh, the monkeys. They love snake. They clean up afterwards. Every year, Danny Ren—'Big Man' in English—brings in the animal of the year. You should see it when it's Tiger year." He honked like it was the year of the Goose. "He puts a baby tiger inside and all the women in the mall want to come in to pet it. Best year for business."

"What does he do for a dragon," I asked, challenging him with a grin.

He belly-laughed and said, "Come back and see."

I might. Maybe I should imitate that idea in my office. On second thought, my office staff would resign if I had a bunch of monkeys or dogs, or God forbid, rats in cages in my office. I'd have to make do with photos or little statues in Clement. Every year, I'd give a Year of the Whatever Animal promotional statue to our customers, emblazoned with our logo.

*Big thoughts. Someday maybe they'll pay off.*

We pushed through clacking bamboo strips hung across a doorway into a room about the size of my office back in Clement. Behind the far wall, which was glass from floor to ceiling, was a forest scene, thick, smooth tree trunks, broad leaves, ferns, trails of moisture running down inside the glass.

The man disappeared while Woo and I sat down in thickly upholstered chairs across the room from the jungle diorama.

"Relax, Charlie," Woo said. His face shone in the dim light seeping into the room. He sat lightly in his chair, leaning forward almost eagerly.

"What's going on, Woo?"

"Our lucky night, Charlie. Mr. Meng said spare no expense. Huan went to get us the finest snake in the house."

Huan and another man emerged from the doorway beside the aquarium. Huan backed into the room, bracing himself against the floor, pulling the tongue of a long wooden wagon with three-foot high sides and wide rubber wheels. The other man bent over, his arms locked straight, palms against the rear wall, straining to push the cart ahead. Water, or some mysterious fluid, dripped from the cart's seams.

Grinning at the snake handler, Woo bounced up from his chair, and I followed him over to the cart. Inside, a huge snake lay tangled, embracing itself, bulging against the side walls, bowing the thin planks. Its body was the color of a faded red barn tattooed with rows of brown footballs. A head the size of a large cantaloupe with open silver eyes lay passively on top of the glittering mound of its body.

I'd never seen anything like it. "God, where did they get that thing?"

"They raised it. From an egg. Takes years."

"What is it? I've never heard of a snake this big."

"Anaconda. Lives in the water and eats deer and wild pigs."

The men tugged and pushed the cart toward the store's front room. Huan snapped something to the man in the rear and Woo laughed. "Stay back, Charlie. Don't get too close to the head. It could grab you with its jaws and wind itself around your neck."

I jumped back. Shades of my worst nightmare as a kid. I'm strolling along a shady sidewalk and a snake drops out of a tree and strangles me to death. As soon as I spooked, the three Chinese burst into belly laughs. More cultural confusion. As long as My Chinese associates found me funny and laughed, I didn't mind. That showed their pleasure in my company, even if in their provincial minds, they thought me an idiot.

"Just kidding, Charlie. It's not hungry," he said, between snorts. The three of them giggled like junior high girls talking with a high school hunk. "It just ate, last year." He said something in Chinese and they all burst out laughing again.

"What's so funny, Woo?"

Woo eventually settled down while the two tittering men resumed maneuvering the cart ahead and out the door. "It's not really funny, but this is the biggest snake in Taipei. None of us thought we'd ever be so lucky to taste such a wonder. We're happy."

Addiction, I thought. Some way to get high. "What do you mean, 'It ate last year'?"

"This one eats every year or two, maybe a pig, a deer. One big supper holds it for a long time."

I'd heard plenty about snake blood aphrodisiacs so I prepared myself to join in the fun with Woo. If I drank the blood, I would redeem myself with Meng. He probably thought I couldn't get it up in the barbershop. Maybe that's why he avoided serious business talk at dinner with Sun. So he sent Woo to get me a libido booster, a shot of self-confidence—this honor I would never refuse, no matter how woozy drinking blood might make me feel. I'd eaten weirder things, though there in the snake shop, I couldn't remember what they were. Fried ants and chocolate-covered African termites, once.

Woo and I entered the main room. Half the store's patrons had their arms around the snake, tugging and hoisting it onto a long wooden table. The other customers or congregants—I didn't really know which—gathered around, speaking rapidly, their voices rising. They pointed at the snake, glancing at me, everyone grinning.

"He must be twenty feet long," I said, astonished to see it stretched to full length. About ten feet from its head, a man hugged the beast against his chest, barely stretching his arms around the snake's body. "How big is he?"

Woo turned to the giant standing at the foot of the table and asked. The giant nodded, folding his hands, and stared at the animal that now lay across the table, rolling its muscles in slow shudders. One of the men picked up a pail and doused the snake with water from its tail to its head. He did it a second time. After the second pail, the snake stopped moving, except for its head that it raised and aimed straight at me.

Everyone fell still and gazed at the snake. I dragged my eyes away from it and examined my fellow snake aficionados, trying to sense what was going on. Some stared with gleams in their eyes, others seemed to be in trances, rocking back and forth on their toes.

The giant said something to Woo. He turned to me and said, "Seven meters. A hundred twenty kilos. He's in his prime."

The handlers stabilized the animal on the table, each man holding it in place with both of his hands. Huan motioned for me to come to him at the head of the table, where he held the sides of the snake's head between his palms. The snake kept its dull eyes fastened on me.

Woo nodded, encouraging me to go on. Moving to the opposite end of the table, near the giant, he clutched the snake's languid tail. Huan pointed his chin first at me, then at a stainless steel pail about the size of a two-quart blender canister. As I held the pail, it reeked of organic rot and my palms squashed moist hunks of goo that stuck to its sides.

"Stand in front of the head," Woo told me. "Hold the bucket under the edge of the table. He'll chop off the head and when it drops, you catch the blood from the neck. You might need more pails." He pointed to several stainless pails stacked on a stool beside me.

"When Huan signals, take the first drink. You're the guest of honor. Hand it around, starting with Huan."

I felt like I was on stage with the audience crowding closer, focusing on me and Huan and the anaconda while the snake and I stared, baffled round eye to passive elliptical eye. Huan raised a cleaver in both hands, stood on his tip toes and reached as high overhead as he could.

Everyone in the room inhaled roughly as the snake opened its massive jaws and squirmed, stretching its daggery mouth toward me. Its tongue flicked out, rasping my chin. I jerked back.

The cleaver fell, smashing into the table with a thunk. The anaconda's severed head shot up into the air, flipped over and landed, mouth agape, on the top of my head. I screamed, dropping the pail, digging the fingers of one hand into the snake's bleeding neck at the base of the head and pushing at its nose with the other. The snake's jaws clenched my head, its teeth stabbing into my ears. I felt the front of my pants become wet and warm. I went blind.

Shouts in Chinese erupted and Woo screamed in English. "Charlie, wait. Stop."

Someone grabbed my hands, fighting with me to pull them away from the head. The jaws let go and the snake head rose up, scraping the back of my scalp and ripping hair out. Slime and blood flowed down my forehead and cheeks and I opened my eyes into the cold blue light of the room. I turned to find a towel to wipe off my face and slipped. My feet slid out from under me flipping me onto on my back, somehow twisted halfway under the table. For an instant before a shower of blood sprayed my chest and face, running into my mouth, the lights dimmed and I felt myself lying on my back in warm water at the river with my kids splashing and laughing.

I swallowed, choking on the thick warm liquid. Scrambling and flailing, I tried to stand up.

Woo screeched and suddenly the rain of blood stopped and I was three feet in the air, hanging upside from Big Man's paws. I swabbed my eyes with my sleeve and arched my neck up. Woo knelt in a shiny pool beside the table legs, his pants and shirt stained black, steadying the bucket as it filled with blood gushing from the snake's neck.

Huan stared at me, his mouth as wide open as the snake's jaws, the cleaver raised, frozen in the air, as if he were fending off an attack. The men holding the snake's convulsing body had their eyes closed, murmuring guttural sounds over and over. The other customers stood in shocked silence, gaping, except for a woman who had the presence of mind to snatch another pail and, standing beside Woo, waited to catch the essence of the snake when Woo's pail overflowed.

The giant grunted and dropped me on my back onto one of the drinking tables, breaking the spell. The rest of the people swooped down to the floor beside the butchering table and began lapping at the puddle of blood that spread in rivulets across the tiles. Woo shouted at them but they ignored him.

Huan snatched the pail from Woo's hands and throwing his head back, he poured blood broth into his mouth, gargling before he swallowed. When he finished, blood dripping from his grinning lips, his shirt splattered, he handed the bucket to Woo.

Woo glanced at me, closed his eyes and raised the bucket to his mouth. He pulled and pulled on the blood, deep gurgling swallows. He finished, grunted and leaned back against the table, his white clothes crimsoned and soggy and offered me the pail. I raised it to my mouth and sipped.

The blood tasted like my own blood that I'd licked from cuts, but with a sweet and gamey note. It smelled a little like boiled chicken that had sat out of the refrigerator too long. I started to set the bucket on the table, but Woo signaled for me to drink more. With his head tilted to the side like a listening bird, Big Man watched me, no doubt wondering what my next strange move would be.

I lifted the pail up and tilted it against my lips. I opened my mouth and the warm soup surged against my throat, almost gagging me. I tipped the pail back to stop the flow and swallowed as gracefully as I could. Glancing at the giant, I saw him smile, and for good measure, I gulped again.

Everyone, except Woo and the giant and me, knelt on the floor. The snake had fallen off the table and its body lay like a fire hose, leaking blood out of its decapitated end. A man tried to prop a bucket under the gash, but he couldn't hold the snake in his blood-greased hands. Two women squatting at the shore of the scarlet blood pond used their hands to brush blood into wide-mouthed glasses, flicking the blood so quickly their fingers blurred.

Huan and Woo lunged toward me, reaching for the half-empty pail in my hands. Woo slipped and spun around, landing on his butt right at my feet. Huan glared, aghast, appealing to the giant to do something.

At the sight of Woo's pratfall, a roar of laughter erupted from my belly, convulsing my shoulders and neck. Big Man joined in, honking and huffing at the mess. Woo tried to jump up, slipped down again, and let himself fall into hilarious laughing at his predicament. The whole crowd screamed and howled. I'd never had such a good time in my life.

We pointed at each other and bayed, unable to stop. Woo finally got up and lurched over to me. "Are you okay?"

"Woo, you're crazy," I shouted. "This is what I've been waiting for." I was feeling drunk and free, having a wild adventure in Taipei.

He clapped me on the back in the first display of affection I'd ever felt from a Chinese man. "Mr. Meng was right about you." I placed the blood bucket on the floor.

Big Man handed me a towel and lumbered to the front of the store where a group had gathered outside to watch the gory melee. He shooed them away and rolled down the aluminum overhead door. He turned to our blood-soaked clan and muttered something. The people stopped talking.

Woo translated. "'Settle down. Stand by the wall.'"

We all watched the giant step carefully into the bloody goo already beginning to clot into a pudding. We all dreaded what could happen if he slipped onto his duff. He gracefully picked up the bucket by its handle, hefted the snake carcass onto his shoulder, laid it out straight as a post on the table, and grumbled to Huan.

Woo managed to retrieve the snake's head from the browning pool under the table. He offered it to me. The scaly flesh hung slack under dull eyes. Its jaws were jammed open showing dozens of bloody teeth with thin strings of spittle dripping from the corner of the mouth. I noticed that the strings were my hairs hanging like lo mein noodles from the decapitated head, my stomach surged and I turned away, closing my throat and holding the souring blood in my craw.

Big Man herded the other customers out of sight into the back room and returned with fresh black towels to Woo and me. Woo began stripping and told me to do the same. We swiped our bodies with the cloth, rubbing off most of the blood. A funk settled in my nose. I blew hard into the towel a half a dozen times, but the stink of fruity meaty decay clung.

Huan had stayed at the table, blood clotting on his face and clothes, butchering the snake with the same cleaver he'd use to behead it. As I toweled the blood off my back and chest, I watched him slice the snake's belly and spread the skin, revealing shiny blue-gray guts. He dug his fingers in, then slipped his arm deep into the entrails and vibrated the body. When he removed his arm, he dragged out a slithery, magenta hunk of organ meat the size of a football.

Lifting the organ in both hands like a priest raising a chalice, Huan called to the owner. The giant nodded impassively. Huan set the organ down on the table and cut off several finger-like chunks with quick expert slashes.

Woo whispered without moving his lips, "The liver."

Wrapped only in our towels, Woo and I approached the table along with the owner. Following Woo's lead, I picked up one of the julienned slices of anaconda liver, tipped back my head and gulped. I flashed back to the time when I was a boy and had swallowed an earthworm. The worm had been cold and rough, but the liver was warm and slipped down my throat like a smooth consommé of fresh tofu.

My snake-munching mates stood around the table, eyes closed, chewing, relishing the oily magic in their mouths. I wished I could enjoy the ceremony as much as they did. I felt another stomach spasm. The last thing I wanted to do was to spew and lose total face with the Chinese. I shut my eyes and counted my breaths, exhaling through my mouth.

When I'd calmed my guts down, I opened my eyes. All three Chinese, including the giant, sagged against the butcher table, their glazed eyes barely open.

They roused themselves while Huan slowly went back to the butchering. The giant offered Woo and me a pile of black silk which, when we unraveled it, became two huge robes, his

own lounging gowns. We wound the silk around our bodies like swaddling blankets. I stepped into my shoes, squish-
ing cool, clotting blood between my toes. Black anaconda goo
spurted out of Woo's shoes. I mimicked his indifference, ignoring my last little discomfort for the sake of group unity in our
Taoist bacchanal.

The giant escorted us to the front of the store and rolled up
the door. He handed Woo a package and bowed. Chuckling, he
shook our hands. He patted me on my head and tugged on my
ears with both hands. A huge laugh erupted from his mouth,
spraying drops of pink saliva into my face.

Woo and I laughed, politely, and, feeling energized, we
nearly jogged back to the street where the Benz was parked,
each musing to ourselves. I wiped the giant's spit off my face.
A rancid, garlic smell had insinuated itself into the stench that
occupied my nose.

"I never did anything like that before," I commented to my
groggy guide who sprawled against the hood of the Benz.

"Nobody in all history ever did that before," Woo said. "I
never had such fun either."

"I've been mostly a vegetarian for so long, I hope I can digest
that raw meat."

"Charlie, you worry too much. The snake blood will take
care of you better than drugs or health food."

As much as I love Chinese mysticism, I didn't want to get
into any discussion of snake magic at two in the morning. My
stomach felt queasy, my head had begun to ache, I felt dizzy,
and my back throbbed. I just needed to get back to my room
and sleep off the night of smoke and blood.

"What's in the package?" I said more to distract myself from
my nausea than out of real curiosity.

"The liver," he hesitated. "For Mr. Meng."

I'd expected something like that.

"Mr. Meng gets half, Big Man gets one third. They give us
the rest. Like profit sharing in America. Generous men."

We rode in silence for a long time. I forced myself to pay strict attention to my breathing. If I let my mind stray, I knew I'd vomit snake blood all over the back seat of the Mercedes.

"That's all Big Man eats," Woo said out of the shadows. "Boa liver, viper liver, red belly liver. He never gets soft. He can have a hundred girls and still keep going. He's number one snake man in Taiwan."

I listened, trying not to make a snide remark. Stories of the sexual powers of these men bored me. Or did they frighten me? No wonder the Chinese are so populous. Did the Taiwanese sublimate a boundless sex drive into their manic business dealing?

"Woo, forgive me for asking?" I saw his eyes open. "About how much does one anaconda like that cost?"

He grunted. "More than you and I have. Feeding the snake for so many years is very expensive. For us, this was a once in a lifetime chance."

How much could pigs and deer cost? I wondered. Should I ask him what all the snakes eat? I didn't want to know. What do I owe Meng now?

"You should know about Big Man, Charlie. He's a hero to us Taiwanese. Did you know Big Man nursed Deng Xiao Peng in his last year?"

"You mean the guy who turned China into the economic power it is? Didn't this Deng die quite a while ago?"

"Not too long by our standards, less than twenty years ago," Woo said. "All Chinese know Deng is the one who set us on the road to riches."

That sounded like the common wisdom the media touted, but what did I care?

Woo went on. "Back then, China gave the president of Taiwan permission to fly Big Man to Beijing. Very smart move for Taiwan. Big Man kept Deng alive when doctors could barely help him breathe. That was when Beijing assured Taiwan we'd always be free partners in wealth."

"Oh?" I said. "Did he bring snakes with him?"

"No. Beijing has good snakes. Big Man stayed more than a year in the Imperial Palace, treating the old man. At ninety-two, Deng died with three girls in his bed and a happy smile on his face. The last thing before he gave up his spirit, Deng held Big Man's hand and said, 'Thank you, Big Man.'

"China was so grateful for Deng's last year with Big Man, they sent Taiwan five shipping containers of ancient treasures. They're in the National Museum. It really pissed off the next generation.

"Truth is, Deng was going to live to 105 before he started getting sick when he was 90 or so. He suspected his juniors were carrying out the ancient Chinese change of dynasty ritual. That's why he called in Big Man. Snake blood neutralizes most poisons, you know."

I didn't know, but that gave me a new business idea.

I noticed my back felt better. It felt normal. I sat up straight.

What if I packaged and marketed snake blood medicine? It's a libido enhancer, a longevity producer. I could have it dried and vacuum packed. It sounds weird, but it's a perfect global business of the future.

Who'd have thought snake blood—a billion dollar business in Asia alone? Something American Tofu will never be, no matter how popular Soy to the World makes it.

*Forget it, Greer. Animal rights people would have your head. First things first. Get the Chief out of your life or maybe you end up dead.*

Ah, Jiminy. You're too right, too often.

I slumped down into the car seat, feeling blood medicine rumbling in my stomach. In 36 hours I'd be home, with a chance to get things back under control. We're coming into the Year of the Rooster. With a little luck, I'll be crowing my success from the rooftops of Manhattan.

*Go ahead, Charlie, enjoy your bliss, forget your woes. But the Chief's still here. Better stay on your toes.*

*The End*

*Book One*

*Blood Medicine*

*The story continues in*
Book Two: The Special Fruit Company
*by Thomas Timmins*

# Chapter One

## *Genevieve O'Connor*

# A CAREER CHANGE

By Thanksgiving of the year I joined American Tofu, my ten-year old son Liam and I were down to our last four hundred dollars. The job at the newspaper had ended when the owner's hand strayed one time too often.

I'd come to Clement the spring before because I needed a change from my old life on Cape Cod. *Winny's of Wellfleet*, my best friend's art gallery that I'd managed for five years, was closing its doors for good in March. Jason, the man who came closest to being the love of my life, left me six months earlier. I spent endless hours sitting in front of my fireplace during the lonely, barren winter, dreaming about our future, wondering what I had to do to make sure Liam had everything he needed.

Liam and I would need a bigger place soon. He needed a lot more space at home than I could give him in our one and a half bedroom apartment. But if I gave it up, I doubted that I could find an affordable year-round apartment, or, dream of dreams, a house anywhere I'd want to live on the Cape.

We moved to P-town when Liam was two. He loved the town, the people, his friends. He swam and sailed every summer and played hockey on the ponds in winter. My friends had become our family. Liam had more women uncles and men aunts than any other child I knew.

My life there had been great for seven years. When Jason split, he took my enthusiasm for P-town life with him. If *Winny's* had stayed open, maybe I'd have postponed our leaving, maybe not. If I was going, Liam was at the perfect age to make a school change, before the cliques started forming in middle school and while he was still too young to feel I'd ruin his life by forcing him to leave his friends.

I told Winny I planned to leave Provincetown.

"It's time, Winny. I can't hang around P-town forever waiting for my boat to come in. I need to try something different. Besides, Liam needs to go be a teenager in a regular town."

"Makes me too sad, Hon. I'll miss you too much."

Tears came to his eyes. I started crying and leaned into him.

"Liam in a normal town? He'll be so bored. God, G, we'd take a lot better care of Liam's manhood in P-town than those manipulative little girls and those violent little boys out there in that decadent straight world. Not to mention those slimy pedophiles sneaking around."

I laughed. He hugged me.

"You? You're another story. I love you and want you to have the maximum best this life can give you."

Whatever my motives for leaving, Winny was my friend. He persuaded his uncle in the rural upstate New York town of Clement to hire me as graphics manager for his newspaper.

"It's beautiful in upstate New York, honey," Winny said. "If you want normal, Clement's middle name is 'Boresville.' I should know. I lived there sixteen lonely years before I got the guts to let my high school drama teacher take me to the city. I never looked back."

"I could use small town boredom for a while, Winny. I'll meet somebody."

"You always do."

Winny took both my hands and put them to his cheeks. "My advice, little sis? Come back here by next summer."

I ignored Winny's pessimism. He didn't want to lose us, but I was determined to make it work out in Clement.

***

After two months in my new town, I lost the newspaper job, my first straight job in years.

When Winny's brainless and resolutely heterosexual uncle's hand brushed my breasts the second time—the first I'd let go as his clumsiness—I erased the day's advertising layout five minutes before deadline and walked out. Standing in front of the newspaper office that afternoon, all I wanted was to get in my car, pick up Liam, and flee to the Cape.

Instead, I drove to the park at the edge of town and sobbed. I had no friends, no love, and now, no job.

The inland skies over Clement barely glowed. The thin light sunk into the earth, clutched it like a fearful mother, spreading a greenish shadow over everything.

I couldn't let myself fall into self-pity. I told myself I just needed time to establish a stable life for Liam and time to find some new friends for myself.

Liam and I decided to rent a house at the lake for the summer. We'd keep our apartment in town, but spend most days and nights at the lake. We'd garden, swim, sail, and plan our next move. I calculated that my savings would last until at least the end of the year when I'd have to find a job. We moved to a three-room cabin on the lake with a view through oaks and cottonwoods out over placid blue water.

Liam said, "Mom, I'm glad we're here. We have to recharge our batteries. I like Clement, but sometimes I feel lonely. It'll take us a while to settle in. I'm sure when school starts up I'll make lots of friends."

I didn't know whether I should be grateful for having such a wise son, or sad because he'd grown up so fast and shouldn't really know his mother so well.

I'm not complaining. I'd never complain about Liam and me. Moan and groan, a little, that's healthy enough. I'm just so deeply in love with my son, it scares me. Not in any bizarre incestuous way, just a pure love that colors every corner of my life and sings to me when I'm hurting. I joy in my mothering of Liam. A lot of times I think, I don't matter, except for Liam—that scares me, too.

Still, I can't imagine a life with any less love. It's odd, backwards, somehow, but I feel this total freedom that comes from my mother love. I've never felt that kind of freedom with a man, maybe because I've never surrendered to a man the way I give in, in my bones, to mothering.

If I ever met a man who makes me feel even freer, even more myself, he's the one who will sweep me away. The one time since Liam was born the right man came close, he split. I've come to wonder if I'm too much for a man. Too independent, too free, too much a mother.

When we came to Clement, I put my desire for a man on the back burner. We'd come for Liam's teenage years, and I'd still be in my thirties when he left for college. That gave me plenty of time to meet somebody.

Maybe living in Clement, without a man calling every day, wouldn't get lonely, but I doubted that. All my life, I'd kept some relationship simmering, if for nothing more than to keep myself company. The way I could keep myself from rushing into something with a man was to accept loneliness as a regular visitor. It would be good for my character, but terrible for my sex life.

Liam and I enjoyed the lake so much that the summer disappeared before I'd had a chance to find a steady income. We rented a sailboat and sailed every day. In rain, we rowed across the lake, unless we heard thunder. I met plenty of single fathers of his lake friends and uncles and married dads' best buddies. I went out every week, but not one interested me enough to have dinner with him a second time.

***

Once we came back from the lake in time for school, I looked seriously for a job, never expecting how hard it would be. The possibility I'd end up clerking in a grocery store, office temping, pizza delivering, or night managing the downtown McDonald's depressed me enough that I almost called the jerk at the newspaper and asked for my job back.

A job managing the local frame shop and art supply store opened up in mid-November. It paid barely enough to cover our rent and food, but I needed to find something before the snow fell. They offered me the job, and I said I'd let them know after Thanksgiving.

Then I met Nora at the Salvation Army Thanksgiving Day dinner where Liam and I had volunteered to help serve the needy.

Nora was friendlier than the average Clem citizen, and she took a liking to Liam, praising him for his generosity and civic sense. Of course, he had no idea what she was talking about. As far as he knew, we were simply doing what we always did on Thanksgiving. We'd started serving up spuds and breasts at the "Salvo" five years before in Wellfleet when we had no place else to celebrate Turkey Day.

Nora was petite, raven-haired, shapely, pretty but not striking. Her face was kind, totally wrinkle-free, she looked thirty. She dressed conservatively but expensively, though you probably couldn't tell unless you knew fabric as I did. Her two most arresting features were her slightly bulging royal blue eyes that looked at you as if you were the most important person in the world. And she listened like a born therapist. When she told me that she was six years older than me, I complimented her on her complexion. She claimed it was her vegetarian diet that kept her looking so young.

As she scooped potatoes, I sliced and forked out the white meat. Liam stood proudly at the end of the table, waving his spatula and talking non-stop as he served the apple and pumpkin pies.

Usually I'm reserved with new people. In Clement, where everyone knew everyone else, reserve was a survival tactic for a single woman. But with Nora, in between filling plates and joking with the diners, I jabbered on about my money situation, my newspaper boss's fondling, my fears for Liam, my artist's life on the Cape.

She told me that she painted and asked me to look at her work sometime.

"Maybe you can you tell me if it's worth trying to sell."

"It's always worth trying," I said. "I don't have to see it to say that. I don't know if I can tell you, but I'd like to see your work. It can be great and not sell."

I was starving for the company of artistic spirits. She was the first artist I'd met since I left the Cape.

She pulled me away from the table as soon as the last guest had received her turkey and gravy. I told Liam to go ahead and sit down to eat, I'd be right back. He'd met some new kids, so while he enjoyed his first Thanksgiving away from Massachusetts, Nora and I sat in the chaplain's office and I told an abbreviated version of my life's story.

When I finished, she took my hand and said, "Go see my husband Monday. We have a food company and he needs a salesperson desperately. You'd be perfect, Genevieve."

My heart leapt, but I doubted the job was for me.

"I've never sold anything but art," I said.

She grinned. "Hey, if you can sell art, selling tofu's gonna be a piece of cake...tofu cheesecake." She laughed and stood up. "Let's go have our pumpkin pie. I'll tell Charlie all about you. Really. Call him."

She didn't worry about my looks, so I assumed she had a solid marriage. I hoped we would become friends. I needed a good friend.

## The author

Thomas Timmins has published and performed his poetry and short fiction in person and in print across the U.S. and on the internet. He founded Fractals, a literary tabloid, cofounded and ran Poets & Players, a performance venue, developed and taught writing and coaching programs for inmates, published commercial writing, and founded and managed small businesses ranging from soyfoods to ice cream to telephone fundraising to biological pest control to a video game start-up to energy efficiency retrofits and a media company.

www.thomastimmins.com